WHITE
BIRD

ALSO BY R. J. PALACIO

Wonder

365 Days of Wonder

Auggie & Me: Three Wonder Stories

White Bird: A Graphic Novel

Pony

WHITE BIRD

A NOVEL

A
WONDER
STORY

R. J. PALACIO

with ERICA S. PERL

ALFRED A. KNOPF 🐎 NEW YORK

Text copyright © 2022 by R. J. Palacio
Illustrations copyright © 2019 by R. J. Palacio
Afterword copyright © 2019 by Ruth Franklin
Text by Erica S. Perl, adapted from the graphic novel by R. J. Palacio
Inking by Kevin Czap

Jacket and Insert: Motion Picture Artwork © 2022 Lions Gate Entertainment Inc. All Rights Reserved.
Photo Credit: Larry Horricks

Glossary image credits are located on page 259.

"Fourth Elegy: The Refugees," from The Collected Poems of Muriel Rukeyser. Copyright © 2005 by Muriel Rukeyser. Reprinted by permission of ICM Partners.

Visit us on the Web! rhcbooks.com

Educators and librarians, for a variety of teaching tools, visit us at RHTeachersLibrarians.com

Library of Congress Cataloging-in-Publication Data is available upon request.
ISBN 978-0-593-56693-0 (trade) — ISBN 978-0-593-56694-7 (lib. bdg.) —
ISBN 978-0-593-56695-4 (ebook)

The text of this book is set in 12-point Seria Pro.
Interior design by April Ward

Printed in the United States of America
10 9 8 7 6 5 4 3 2 1
First Edition

For Mollie, her ancestors,
and her descendants
—R.J.P.

For all those who spread
their wings, shelter others,
and soar toward peace
—E.S.P.

They are the children.   They have their games.
They made a circle on a map of time,
skipping they entered it, laughing lifted the agate.
I will get you an orange cat, and a pig called Tangerine.
The gladness-bird beats wings against an opaque glass.
There is a white bird in the top of the tree.
They leave their games, and pass.

> —Muriel Rukeyser, "Fourth Elegy: The Refugees"

PROLOGUE

Those who cannot remember the past
are condemned to repeat it.
—George Santayana

PRESENT DAY

"Julian, no more video games. Do your homework."

Julian's eyes stayed fixed on the screen of his phone. "This is homework," he replied. "I'm FaceTiming Grandmère for my humanities project."

Julian's mother raised an eyebrow. Her son rarely called his grandmother for any reason, and this was the first she was hearing of a school project. She was tempted to see if Julian was pulling a fast one on her. But then she heard the sound of the call ringing on the other end, so she left the room and closed the door. The phone continued to ring, and Julian was about to hang up and start another video game when he heard a familiar voice answer.

"Allô? Allô?"

A face swam into view. It was Grandmère, all right. Julian's grandmother showed few signs of slowing down as she got older. For her, it was a point of pride. Bright lipstick and chic clothing told the world that she remained a force to be reckoned with. So did her tendency to speak her mind. She was a woman of strong opinions.

1

"Hey, Grandmère!" replied Julian.

"Allô?" came back in response. "Allô? Julian, is that you?"

Of course, she knew it had to be Julian—no one else called her Grandmère. To the rest of the world, she was Madame Albans or Sara. She poked at the screen in frustration, able to hear but not see her grandson. Despite her best efforts, technology seemed to look for ways to betray her. Sometimes the inadvertent push of a wrong button would end the call completely. Other times, the caller would sound like he was at the bottom of a well. This was not entirely unexpected when the caller lived in New York City, as Julian did. After all, an ocean separated his home from her apartment in Paris.

"Grandmère, you have to look into the phone!" Julian instructed her. "And put your glasses on!" he added.

Dutifully, she did, and was rewarded by the sight of her grandson's sweet brown eyes. At least, one of them. The boy needed his hair cut, she noticed. Julian's bangs hung over his eyebrows, obscuring his handsome young face. Had they been in the same room, she might have reached over and brushed them out of the way with her hand. She might even have taken him to her hairdresser, Marcel, for a quick trim. But with all the miles separating them, she chose to ignore his mop top and focus instead on the fact that her grandson was calling her—a rare treat.

"Oh! There you are!" she said brightly. "I see you now. Allô, mon cher! How are you? How is the new school?"

Her question was weighted with meaning. Julian had recently transferred schools, and not for the best of reasons. The idea was to give him a chance at a fresh start. Whether that would actually happen was mostly in Julian's hands, and they both knew it.

"It's okay. I like it," he said. "I mean, I miss Beecher Prep and all. But I still feel really bad about . . . well, you know . . ." He looked away for a moment, as if trying to find the words. Or perhaps lost in a memory.

". . . some of the stuff I did," he finally said.

His grandmother's heart went out to him. She had learned some of the details of his disastrous fifth-grade year from her son and his wife, who had been quick to blame others. They claimed that there had been incidents—misunderstandings, really, to hear them tell it—and that the school had let several children off the hook, but not Julian. It was not until a family trip to Paris that the full details came out. Julian told his grandmother a different story from the one his parents had shared—one in which Julian was less of a victim and more of an active participant in all that had transpired. His sense of remorse impressed his grandmother. It also gave her hope that her grandson might be ready to take full advantage of the fresh start he had been offered.

Julian propped his elbow on the table, leaned into his hand, and sighed. "Sometimes I wish I could go back in time. Or have a do-over, you know?"

Grandmère nodded. She wanted to reach through the phone and hug him. For, of course, she knew only too well.

"Oh yes, mon cher," she told him. "We all have those kinds of regrets. Just remember: we are not defined by our mistakes, but by what we do after we've learned from them. D'accord?"

Julian shook his hair out of his eyes, and his grandmother noticed a wave of relief pass across his face.

"Okay, Grandmère. Thanks," he said. "I'm actually calling you today because of school. I have a project for my humanities class. I'm supposed to write an essay about someone I know, and I want my essay to be about you."

"Me? I'm so flattered!" replied Grandmère. She found it humorous that young people often assumed their elders to be out of step, out of touch, and out of fashion. "When, in fact," she had said to Julian on more than one occasion, "we have lived long enough to see that everything your generation thinks of as new is simply a recycled version of something we've seen many times before."

But then her grandson said something even more surprising.

"I want to share your story, from when you were a little girl, during the war."

"Hmm, I see," Grandmère said quietly.

Julian began talking quickly, sensing her reluctance. "I want to write about you and Tourteau, Grandmère," he said. "I know you told me the story already, the last time I visited you. But this time I'd like to record you. And I was thinking, maybe you could give me more details."

"Hmm . . . ," Grandmère said again. She was trying to make up her mind. Julian was right, of course. She had long wanted to tell him the whole story of her past, once he was old enough to hear it. On his most recent visit to Paris, the right moment had finally come. And yet, as important as it felt to share her past with her grandson, she had stopped short of telling him everything. She'd held back some of the pieces, just for herself.

Is he ready for me to share all of it? she wondered. And am I?

"Oh, Julian," she said, trying to figure out how to explain her complicated feelings. It felt strange to be at a loss for words. "This is a lovely idea," she finally said, "but . . . it's hard for me to talk about these things."

"I'm sorry," replied Julian, worry flashing in his eyes. "I didn't mean to upset you," he added. "It's okay. We don't have to—"

And in that moment, Grandmère decided. It wasn't that she was moved by his wanting to spare her the pain of reliving the memories. It was actually the opposite—his willingness to say forget it and shift the conversation to more pleasant topics gave her the nudge she needed.

"No," she said firmly. "We should talk about it, mon cher. Even if it is hard. In fact, because it is hard. Because your generation needs to know these things."

She paused, took off her glasses, and rubbed her eyes. Fine, she told herself. I'll do this. But—how?

"All right," she continued, replacing her spectacles and trying to shake off the sensation of walking through fog. There was a path here, somewhere, but could she find it without a road map? "I will tell you the story, Julian. The whole story, even the parts I have never told anyone before."

"Are you sure, Grandmère?" asked Julian.

"Yes, mon cher. I am," she told him, trying to project a confidence she didn't quite feel. "Julian, those were dark times, absolutely. Yet what has stayed with me the most for all these years is not the darkness but the light. That is the story I want to share with you."

She took a deep breath.

" 'Once upon a time' is how most fairy tales begin," Grandmère explained to Julian. "That is how I will start my story, too, because my life truly began as a fairy tale. I wasn't a princess, and I didn't live in a palace or have a closet full of silk ball gowns, mind you. But, looking back, I had everything that mattered and more. Much more."

She took a sip of water. And then she poured herself a small glass of red wine. "I grew up in a town called Aubervilliers-aux-Bois in the French countryside, near the Margeride mountains." She picked up a framed photograph on her desk and toyed with it. The quaint village square depicted on it reminded her of those days. "It was, at the time, a very happy life. I had wonderful parents. A beautiful home. Many friends. Nice clothing. Toys. I even had an upright piano to play, which felt very fancy indeed. To be truthful, I suppose you could say that, well, maybe I was a little spoiled."

"Maybe a little?" teased Julian.

"Maybe a lot," Grandmère admitted. "Yes, yes . . . maybe a lot, mon cher."

Her voice, Julian couldn't help but notice, had taken on a kind of distant air, like she was speaking from somewhere far away. This was true, of course, since Grandmère was quite literally far away. But as she spoke of her past, it felt like she was drifting even farther.

"My father was a surgeon," she continued, so quietly that Julian had to get closer to his phone to hear her. "Dr. Max Blum. He was famous. People came from all over to see him. And my mother was a teacher. She taught math at the university level, which was unheard of in those days—that a woman would teach in a university. But she did. . . ."

She paused, and closed her eyes.

"They were so loving, Julian," she whispered. "They were so, so loving. And in the beginning, their warm embrace kept me from realizing that all around us, things were starting to change."

PART ONE

The birds know mountains that we have not dreamed. . . .
—Muriel Rukeyser, "Fifth Elegy: A Turning Wind"

CHAPTER ONE
1930s, France

"Sara? Sara, are you ready to go?"

I spun around in an exasperated circle, watching the skirt of my new dress flare out. "Papa, how can you ask that? I've been ready for hours," I told him.

"Hours?" He raised a dubious eyebrow.

I nodded. "Yes, hours. Can we go now?"

"In a moment, when your mother is ready. Where's your coat and hat?" asked Papa.

I groaned dramatically. "It's spring, Papa. I don't need my coat and hat."

Papa put on his own coat and hat, then folded his arms across his chest. "My dear girl, I am a man of science. The calendar may say it is spring, but look outside and you'll see that the trees are telling a different story."

"The trees say I'm fine without my coat and hat," I informed him.

"Your mother says otherwise, and that's final," said Maman, joining us in the front hall. She looked so chic in her red wool coat and matching hat that I abandoned my protest and put mine on, too.

"Fine. Can we go now?" I asked, twirling again for her to admire me. She kissed me on the head, and we set off for the market, the three of us, arm in arm.

This was our family tradition on weekend mornings. We would go for a brisk walk together and do our grocery shopping. I always insisted on walking in the middle. I felt safe and snug between the two of them. I also liked imagining the three of us as a sandwich: my tall, elegant papa and my pretty, sophisticated maman were the two sides of *une baguette*, and I was *un petit morceau de fromage* nestled between them.

"Bonjour, Dr. Blum! Bonjour, Madame Blum!" our friends and neighbors would call out as we passed them in the streets. I liked noticing the way the people in our town looked at us. *That's Dr. Blum*, I would imagine them telling visitors. *He's an extremely talented surgeon. And his wife is brilliant as well. She teaches at the university! And she was one of the first women in our village to graduate with an advanced degree in mathematics. Aren't they a handsome couple? That's their daughter, Sara. A lovely child. She plays piano and has many friends and—*

"Sara?"

"Hmm?" I looked up, flustered.

Maman gave me a bemused smile and wagged her finger. "Were you daydreaming again?"

"No! I— Well, maybe," I admitted.

"It's not a crime," Papa assured me. "If anything, it is a

sign of intellect. You have a curious mind, Sara. Just like your mother."

"I think the daydreaming part comes from your father," said Maman.

We continued on our way. As we did, Papa quietly took my right hand. Soon, Maman slipped her hand into my left. I watched hopefully for a knowing glance to pass across my parents' faces. Sure enough . . .

"Un . . . deux . . . trois!" they called, swinging my arms rhythmically before lifting me off my feet. I hopped at just the right moment to take flight, springing into the air. Maman laughed.

"You're getting too big for this, Sara," she chided me.

"Never!" I protested, smiling back. I knew there was some truth in what she said—I wasn't a baby anymore. But I still liked to play, and I wasn't ready to give up our little games. I snatched a loaf of bread from her market basket and dashed off with it, holding the baguette aloft and hoping for a chase.

"Come back here!" called Papa. But he didn't run after me immediately. I could see him whispering to Maman, his brow furrowed. My mother nodded gravely at whatever he was saying, then whispered something back. I wondered what they were talking about. Perhaps Maman thought I shouldn't be running around in my new dress? Or maybe what looked like concern was simply the two of them trying to keep a secret from me. I did have a birthday coming up in May—could they be figuring out the perfect gift?

I studied them, heads together, and made a mental note

to keep an eye out for other clues. That wouldn't be hard to do, because I adored watching them. Theirs was a great love, but also a meeting of the minds. While doctors all over the world sought Papa's advice on important medical matters, his most trusted confidante was not someone in the medical profession—it was Maman.

Within a few minutes, Papa raced after me, all signs of whatever had been preoccupying him forgotten. I shrieked with excitement, ducking to hide behind a tree. Both of us kept darting out and laughing, our chase continuing merrily until Papa triumphantly reclaimed the baguette.

As Papa caught his breath, I seized the moment to follow up on an idea I had had earlier. "Papa, you said it's spring, yes? Can we go to the forest for a picnic?"

"Not quite yet, my little bird," he told me, his eyes sparkling. "But soon, I promise."

The Mernuit forest, near our home, was a dark and scary place, especially for us children. There were legends, going back centuries, about giant wolves that roamed the woods. Elderly people in my village were quick to warn me and my friends not to linger near the woods after dark, on account of wolves. To hear them tell it, these terrifying beasts would slip out unnoticed with the fog, prey on their victims, and leave as silently as they came. I didn't know whether to believe this or not, but I came to view the forest as an ominous place much of the time.

Except in springtime, when something magical happened in the forest. Going to see it was another family tradition—one I looked forward to every year.

A few days later, I asked Papa for a picnic in the woods again. And again, and again, and again, until the day I got the answer I was hoping for.

"Let's ask your maman," he said, smiling. It was finally time.

We packed up a lunch basket. Nothing fancy—just some sandwiches, red wine for my parents, lemonade for me, and some fruit. Maman carefully folded a sky-blue picnic blanket with an embroidered border of pink roses. Then we walked deeper and deeper into the forest. The woods were less terrifying in the light of day, especially with both of my parents beside me. But I still kept a careful eye out for ferocious beasts, just in case.

Happily, the sight that greeted us was not a menacing bank of fog. Or a hungry wolf.

"Bluebells!" I cried, running into the purple vale as if greeting an old friend. The entire forest floor was in bloom, bursting forth in bright blue and violet hues. While my parents set out the picnic, I danced around in the glade. It was beautiful and fragrant beyond my wildest dreams.

"It's magical here," I announced to Maman when I finally was able to tear myself away from playing princess among the fairy flowers. I collapsed in a happy heap next to her on the blanket.

"It certainly feels that way," she allowed. Her mathematical mind was often reluctant to acknowledge circumstances that could not be scientifically validated.

"It is," I insisted stubbornly.

"She's right, you know, Rose," said my papa, topping off my mother's wineglass. I grinned with pleasure that he was taking my side. "Bluebells aren't usually found this far south. Clearly, these flowers were brought here by fairy magic. There's simply no logical explanation."

"Ha! I knew it," I cried with jubilation.

Maman took a sip, raising her free hand in mock defeat. Then she set down her glass and sighed, gazing at me with admiration. "Look at our little girl, Max," she said. "She's getting so big!"

Papa shook his head in protest. "She's still our little bird, Rose."

Little bird. I quickly sprang to my feet at the sound of my father's pet name for me. It was also our code for my favorite game.

"Oh, Papa!" I said. "Can you make me fly?"

"Of course," he replied, getting to his feet and reaching out for me. "How high will you fly?"

"As high as the sky!" I assured him. We locked eyes and I held his face in my hands, reveling in his attention. He was so strong, my papa. There was nothing he could not do.

"And how fast will you go?" he asked.

That was my cue to spread my arms wide as he lifted me up and began to swing me around in a wide circle.

"As fast as a crow!" I proclaimed.

"Then close your eyes . . . ," said Papa, swinging me around. I took a deep breath as I gained momentum. This was my next-to-favorite part—the anticipation that came as I whirled, still secure in his grasp, just barely.

"...Time to rise!" he called, launching me high into the air.

I kept my eyes tightly shut, feeling weightless as I soared into the air. I pictured myself as my father's little bird, the wind catching my wings and lifting me triumphantly skyward. Landing was always a rude awakening for me, but never a painful one. My father was so gentle with his tosses that I never got hurt. Instead, I begged for more.

I loved that game and how it belonged to just us, my father and me.

I loved how it made me feel—happy and carefree as a bird.

I loved knowing that even when he let go, I was completely protected and safe.

CHAPTER TWO
Summer 1940-Fall 1942

"Sara, come take a look at this," called Papa to me one morning. I was standing in our front hall, my book bag already on my shoulder and my hand on the doorknob. "Can you show me later?" I asked. "I'm going to be late for school."

"This will only take a moment," Papa replied. "And it's important. Look here and read what it says."

Impatiently, I glanced at the newspaper he was holding up. His hand was by the newspaper's date, but I knew that wasn't the part he was emphasizing. "France Surrenders to Germany," I read aloud. "Papa, I know about that—we talked about it at dinner last night." And every night, I thought. Of course there was a war going on—everyone knew that. But when Adolf Hitler and the German Nazi Party decided to invade France earlier that month, they took over our nightly family dinner conversations, too.

"Yes, but there's more," said Papa, indicating a map that was printed under the headlines. "This is France. Point to where we live."

I did as I was told. Papa drew a red circle around the location on the map. "Very good," he said. "Now, you see, there are two zones, and our village is located in the Unoccupied, or Free, Zone. This means we are very lucky. We should be grateful that our home is not in the Occupied Zone."

"Why?" I asked.

"Because the Occupied Zone is controlled by Germany. There are, and may continue to be, many changes and disruptions there as a result. But here our lives should continue more or less as normal."

I glanced at the newspaper again, confused. "I thought France surrendered. Doesn't that mean Germany runs everything now?"

He shook his head. "No, that's why there are two zones. Our zone is controlled by a new French government, based in the town of Vichy, not terribly far from here. The new government is working with the Germans but sets its own rules for our zone. I just wanted you to know that, because the things one might see and hear in the streets can be confusing. I want you to keep focusing on your studies and not spend too much time worrying about the war. And if you have any questions, you can always come to me."

"Okay," I said. "Can I go to school now?"

Papa smiled. "You may."

On my way to school, I rode my scooter past soldiers, who were an increasing presence in our town. *Is that what Papa meant?* I wondered. I noticed the big red banners with the black-on-white twisted crosses called swastikas. They represented the Nazi Party, and they had become omnipresent in recent months. Perhaps they, too, were what Papa was referring to. And I saw people greeting each other on the streets with a stiff-armed salute and cries of "Heil Hitler!" instead of "Good morning." It was all a little strange and unnerving. But if this was what Papa was talking about, it meant nothing. And I was inclined to believe him. After all, Papa was an educated man and could speak with authority on any subject. To my mind, he was incapable of being wrong about anything.

A couple of weeks later, I came home from school one day and was surprised to find Maman sitting at the piano. Usually she wouldn't be home from teaching at this hour. I slid onto the bench next to her.

"Shall we play a duet?" I suggested, arranging my hands on the keyboard.

When she didn't respond, I turned my head and looked up at her.

"What's wrong?" I asked.

Maman dabbed at her eyes but did not answer. Reluctantly, she handed me a piece of paper. I read it over quickly, then looked back at her with confusion.

"They're firing you from the university?" I asked. "But—why?"

Maman burst into tears and ran out of the room.

When Papa came home from work, I asked him to explain.

"This isn't about anything she did or didn't do," he told me. "It's the government. Recently, they passed laws forbidding us Jews to work in certain jobs. Including teaching."

"But that shouldn't affect Maman. We live in the Unoccupied Zone," I pointed out.

Papa sighed. "It's complicated, my little bird," he said, looking more tired than usual. "The Nazis have been very successful in blaming Jews for all the troubles throughout Europe," he explained. "They have convinced German citizens to believe these anti-Jewish sentiments, and their message has taken hold throughout France."

In other words, the Nazi soldiers and salutes and banners in the streets weren't the worst of it. They signified something far more insidious than I had realized. Something that was spreading, despite what we had been told about the safety that could be found in the so-called Free Zone. And despite how obvious these lies were, they seemed to be working. Otherwise Maman would still have her job at the university. I wished with all my heart that people would come to their senses and see reason.

But, like anything, I got used to it. War news was everywhere, but for many months I did my best to tune it out. I could still go more or less wherever I wanted on my bike and scooter and play with my friends like a regular kid. Until one day, almost two years later, when a letter arrived in our mailbox.

"Papa, look!" I carried it in to him. "It's from Aunt Simone, in Paris."

"Oh?" He exchanged a quick glance with Maman before opening it.

"Can I read it after you, Papa?" I asked. I was very fond of

Papa's sister and her family. Her son, my cousin Marc, was only a year younger than me.

"It seems like they're trying to come to the Free Zone," he told me and Maman.

"That's wonderful!" I replied. I did the math in my head. I knew we'd last seen them on my seventh birthday, in May 1937. And I had just turned twelve, so . . . more than five years? That didn't seem possible. "They can stay with us, can't they?"

"Of course," said Maman. "If they're able to travel, they're always welcome here."

Papa handed the letter to me.

le 20 juin, 1942

My dear brother,

I wish I was writing to you in happier times. I am sure you have followed the situation in the Occupied Zone in the news, but I must confess that it is far worse than is being reported. We are required to wear yellow cloth stars on our clothing so we can be identified as Jews upon sight. Henri and I have both lost our jobs, money is very tight, and Marc can no longer attend school. Worst of all, we have been hearing rumors of Jewish families being rounded up and removed from their homes—a terrifying thought. We are trying to leave Paris in the hopes of avoiding this fate. I will let you know when we have our

paperwork and finances in order to travel. We don't
want to impose upon you, Rose, and Sara. However,
we have nowhere else to go.

Bises,
Simone

My aunt's letter gave me chills. I hoped they would make it to our village soon. Things were increasingly strange and tense here, but nothing like the situation she described in Paris. I didn't have to wear an ugly yellow star on my coat. I was still able to go to school and play and gossip and laugh with my friends. I continued to try to reassure myself even when, in November, the newspaper reported that the Germans now occupied the Free Zone.

Shortly thereafter, on an unseasonably warm fall day, my friend Mariann turned to me after school.

"Some of us are going to go get ice cream," she said. "Do you want to come?"

"Sure," I said, and happily walked with her and a couple of other girls from our class to the shop. When we got there, the others ran ahead to select their flavors, but a sign in the window caught my eye. Jews are not permitted here, it said.

I stood there, staring at it.

"I realized I left my wallet at home," I told my friends when they emerged with their cones, confused at why I hadn't accompanied them inside.

"I can lend you the money," offered Mariann, holding out her change purse.

"Thanks, but it's fine. I'm actually not hungry," I told her. This was not entirely untrue. The sign in the window had definitely caused me to lose my appetite. She shrugged and we continued to walk together. I felt a wave of relief that none of them had noticed the sign. It made me feel odd and uncomfortable, like the shopkeepers knew something about me that I hadn't even realized myself. Was I bad in some way? Unmannered, or unlikable, perhaps? I didn't think so, but I also didn't know who to ask.

I fell back into laughing with my friends, pushing what had just occurred out of my mind. It's just one store, I told myself. And they're not the only ice cream shop in town. I'll just have to get my ice cream somewhere else! I smiled, picturing the ice cream shop of my dreams. I imagined myself in a glamorous pink party dress, selecting scoop after scoop, until they presented me with a mouthwatering tower of an ice cream cone. At my imaginary ice cream parlor, Jews would be not only permitted but welcomed.

Yet as I walked away with my friends, I couldn't help but feel a sad ache.

Everyone else's ice cream cone was real.

Mine was just make-believe.

"Did your cousin's family end up coming to stay with you?" asked Julian.

"No. Before they could leave Paris, the Vel' d'Hiv roundup happened."

"The Vel' d'Hiv?"

Grandmère hesitated. This was one of the reasons she had resisted telling Julian the whole story. But he had asked, and she had promised to tell him everything. Even the painful parts, like this. "It was a roundup of Jews," she explained. "Like my aunt had feared. In July 1942, over 13,000 people, including 4,000 children, were arrested and held inside a stadium in Paris. The conditions were horrible. No food or water. Families were separated. Then they were put on trains and deported. Some were sent to internment camps in France. Most ended up in concentration camps in the east. Many died."

"That's awful," said Julian. "What about your cousin and his family?"

"I don't know," she replied. "After the Vel' d'Hiv, we never heard from them again."

CHAPTER THREE
Spring 1943

"Sara?"

I could hear Mademoiselle Petitjean calling my name, but just barely. It sounded like my teacher was at the other end of a long beach. Between us stretched a glorious expanse of flowers, leaves, and birds. With a flourish of my pencil, I added another little bird to the scene. I gave it wings and watched it take flight.

"Sara."

Her voice came again, still a million miles away. I was too busy to respond, lost in a world of my own creation. In art class, this was fine. But it was hard for me to keep from drawing in other classes as well. Whenever Mademoiselle Petitjean began our math lesson, I would slide my sketchbook out from its hiding place beneath my textbook. Then, when she wasn't looking, I would wander in.

I couldn't help it! I loved to draw. Birds. Flowers. Leaves. Drawing was my escape from the world. When I drew, I would forget about the war, the Nazis, and everything that was going on around me. I would lose myself in the doodles of my imagination. I would feel my soul take flight. . . .

"Sara!"

"Huh? Yes?"

Mademoiselle Petitjean stood over me, frowning. Embarrassed, I looked down and discovered, to my horror, blatant evidence of my daydreaming: an open sketchbook, filled with page after page of my drawings. My math book was shoved to one side, clearly ignored. I might have my mother's smile, but I did not inherit her passion for mathematics.

"Would you like to share your picture with the rest of the class?" my teacher asked pointedly.

"No, Mademoiselle Petitjean!" I replied. I quickly covered my art with my hands. I prided myself on being considered an attentive student. It was mortifying to have been caught doodling in the middle of a lesson.

I thought I was going to be sick, but then I saw her expression change. She placed a kindly hand on my shoulder and leaned over to confide in me.

"These are very beautiful drawings, Sara. You have a real gift."

"Thank you," I whispered, relief washing over me.

"I know that in the springtime, many students' minds tend to wander. But right now we're doing math, so—"

BRRINNG-BRRINNG!

Her words were interrupted by the bell. The school day was over.

"Lucky you. Saved by the bell. All right, everyone. Class dismissed! See you tomorrow, children!"

Mademoiselle Petitjean held on to my shoulder a moment longer, giving me a parting look that told me not to press my luck again. I thanked her and silently promised that I would honor her kindness by keeping my sketchbook firmly shut for our next math lesson. I loved the École Lafayette, a parochial school that welcomed children of all faiths and provided us with wonderful, supportive teachers like Mademoiselle Petitjean. She was unfailingly encouraging and kind, even when my daydreaming and doodling habits tested her patience.

I grabbed my sweater and dashed out of the classroom to catch up with Mariann and Sophie. I soon joined the throng of children scrambling to leave school as quickly as possible.

Only one boy in our class lagged behind, as he did every day. He was the boy who sat next to me in class. Not by choice, mind you. His last name was Beaumier and mine Blum. So the alphabet dictated that we spend our days side by side. That was the full extent of our connection. I did my best to ignore him.

But he didn't ignore me. And that fact, as well as the fact that he always left after everyone else, ended up proving fortunate for me. Because in my haste to leave that day, I accidentally dropped my sketchbook to the floor.

I didn't realize I had dropped it—I was too mortified by having my teacher catch me doodling, and too eager to catch up with my friends.

But the boy saw my sketchbook on the floor. And he carefully collected it to return it to me.

Had he not, the janitor might have thrown it away. It was the kind of thoughtful thing a friend would do, but I was not this boy's friend. I never spoke to him in class. Or outside of class, for that matter. I didn't even know his real name.

I just knew him by what everyone called him: Tourteau.

"Tourteau? Is that, like, 'turtle' in French?" guessed Julian.

Grandmère shook her head. "La tortue is 'the turtle.' Tourteau means 'crab.' It was a cruel nickname for a boy who had the misfortune of contracting polio as a young child."

Julian looked queasy. "Did he have a face like a crab?"

"Not at all. His face was not affected, and his torso and arms were strong. But when the disease ravaged his body, it left his legs twisted and shriveled. He used crutches to get around."

"Oh," said Julian quietly. "That sounds bad. . . ." His voice trailed off and he looked down. His grandmother knew such things made him uncomfortable, but it wasn't her style to shy away from them. She knew that the problems at his previous school had stemmed from his behavior toward a child with physical differences. In fact, this was why she had told him about Tourteau in the first place, when he'd visited her in Paris. She was glad the story of Tourteau had stayed with him, even if it haunted him a little.

"Yes," she agreed. "It was bad. Things were not easy for him, due to the polio. And for other reasons."

CHAPTER FOUR

No one talked to Tourteau.

But everyone talked about him.

"I heard he caught it from his father" was what Sophie said. She balled up her hand into a twisted fist, hunched her back, and contorted her face into a gargoyle's grimace. Everyone laughed. No one pointed out that, in fact, Tourteau's upper body was just like anyone else's. The disease had affected only his legs.

"I don't think that's how polio works," I said. I made a mental note to ask Papa.

"It's true!" insisted Sophie. "Everyone knows it."

Mariann wrinkled her nose. "I don't know how you can stand sitting next to him, Sara. He smells of *merde*."

"He gets that from his father, too!" added Sophie. "He works in the sewers, and his whole family has to live down there. They have their own special fragrance: *eau d'égoutier*." She pretended to dab fancy perfume behind each ear. "It's all the rage in Paris," she continued. "Try it! You too can smell like a sewer worker." Everyone laughed, including me. After all, the idea of bottling that particular scent was funny.

I wanted to point out that Tourteau did not smell like the sewers. And I doubted that he—or anyone else—actually lived down there. But before I could get up the nerve to open my mouth, I heard a small voice behind me.

"Um . . . excuse me, Sara?"

I glanced over my shoulder and was surprised to find Tourteau, propped up on his crutches, hanging back at the edge of my circle of friends. I felt a flush of guilt, wondering if he had heard us making fun of him.

"Eww. What does he want?" asked Sophie, raising a critical eyebrow.

I shrugged lightly. But as I turned to face him, I noticed that Tourteau was extending a hand toward me. In it was a slim brown notebook.

"You dropped your sketchbook between our desks," he said.

Behind me, Sophie whispered loudly to Mariann, "I can smell him from here."

"Um. Thanks," I said flatly, taking my sketchbook from him. I was genuinely grateful to get it back. But I knew that expressing anything other than disdain would inspire more jokes at his expense. And at mine.

"You're welcome," he replied with a polite bow. Tourteau turned and went on his way. That was the first time I had ever spoken to him, in all the years we had sat beside each other. I quickly turned away, too, only to see the bemused grins on my friends' faces.

"I think he likes you, Sara," teased Sophie.

I made a face. "Eww. Don't say that." Then I laughed at the very idea. Me and Tourteau—how ridiculous would that be? I felt a little pang of guilt. Maman would have been appalled if she could see me acting this way. But she would never know. And besides, it felt like harmless teasing.

"What's in that little book of yours, anyway?" asked Sophie. "Love poems?" She struck a pose, nose in the air. "Oh, my darling... shall I compare thee to a spiny lobster, perhaps? Or, oh, I don't know, a beetle? Mon amour, you and I are—"

"Speaking of poetry," I interrupted, eager to change the subject, "did either of you write down the page numbers for the reading we need to do tonight?"

Mariann opened her notebook to look it up. But before she could give me the assignment, I heard the distinctive sounds of a schoolyard scuffle behind us.

Three older and larger boys surrounded Tourteau. One of them was named Vincent. He was tall and handsome, with blond hair and piercing blue eyes. He was the kind of boy I might have written poems for, if I did that sort of thing. I was not the only girl in my grade with a crush on him, and I'm pretty sure he knew it.

"Go home, sewer rat!" one of the boys said. The others laughed. I told myself that they were just joking around, like my friends and I had done. But their boyish teasing quickly turned into roughhousing.

"Maybe he just needs a little push!" joked Vincent, and the next thing I knew, Tourteau was sprawled on the ground. His cap fell off as he toppled over. Vincent snatched it up and tossed it on top of Tourteau. "Don't forget your hat!" he said.

Then, to my astonishment, Vincent turned and locked eyes with me. Everything was happening so fast, and yet time stood still. My heart started racing as he opened his beautiful mouth and spoke to me for the very first time.

"Hey, what did the little cripple give you, anyway?" he asked.

"My sketchbook," I replied. I could hear Sophie and Mariann murmuring over my shoulder. This was totally unheard of. Handsome, popular older boys like Vincent didn't usually notice little mice like us.

He held out his hand toward me. "Let me see it," he said.

Without a word, I complied. Yes, that book held my private thoughts and dreams—my whole imaginary world. And yet I secretly hoped he'd see the beauty in it. Maybe he'd even compliment my talent, as Mademoiselle Petitjean had.

I held my breath as he flipped through the pages, his friends leaning in to peek.

"Hey, you're a pretty good artist," he finally said, the corners of his mouth curling up in a grin.

"Oh! Thank y—" I started to accept his praise, looking down modestly.

"For a Jew."

The words hit me like a bucket of ice water. Startled, I glanced up, and saw that his smile was now a cruel smirk. He threw my sketchbook on the ground like it was garbage and stalked off without another word. Laughing, his friends followed behind him.

"Sara? Let's get out of here," said Mariann, her hand on my arm.

I stood there silently, a tear rolling down my cheek, feeling as if I had been slapped.

"I should have said something," I finally whispered. In my head, all sorts of possible responses sprang to mind, too late. *You jerk! You ought to be ashamed of yourself, speaking that way to me! I'll bet you can't even draw a stick figure!*

Why had I gone mute? Was I too shocked to respond, or too afraid? It was like the ice cream store incident all over again, only worse. I had a deep and increasingly familiar feeling of worry that perhaps he was right and something was obviously wrong with me.

"Forget about it. He's not worth it," Mariann told me.

I let my friends guide me along, but I felt numb. The sign in the ice cream shop window was upsetting, but it applied to all Jews, not just me. This was so much worse. It was the first time I had ever personally been the target of anti-Semitism.

I felt so humiliated. Angry. Hurt. To be attacked—not for something I had done, but for something I *was*. This was new to me. And it shook me to the core.

"Don't pay attention to Vincent," said Sophie, her arm draped protectively around my shoulders. "He's just a stupid boy. Besides, they say his father works for the Nazis."

I shook my head as if trying to shake off a bad dream. "To think I had a crush on him," I said.

"Just put it out of your mind, Sara," advised Mariann.

Easy for you to say, I thought. *You're not Jewish.*

I could not put it out of my mind. After I said goodbye to my friends, I rode my scooter home, like always. But suddenly the world seemed different. Everywhere I looked, there were signs. Not omens, but actual signs.

I stopped short in front of one in a shop window. The boulangerie, of all places, where my family had purchased loaves of delicious bread for years. Staring back at me was a grotesque creature with evil, menacing eyes and a huge hooked nose. It was a poster for a German film called *Der Ewige Jude*, which meant "The Eternal Jew." I noticed my horrified reflection superimposed on the glass in front of the poster. Was this how my classmates saw me?

I pushed on, going past the cinema where my father and mother sometimes took me. Or rather, used to take me. *Pas de Juifs* said a banner across the ticket window. "No Jews." Just like the sign at the ice cream shop. And everywhere I went, I couldn't escape the sight of those bright red banners flapping in the breeze. When I first saw them, the swastikas reminded me of windmills. But as I learned what they represented, they seemed more like giant fans with sharpened blades, whirring and threatening to cut me if I got too close.

I pushed my scooter faster and faster, trying to push all of these horrible images out of my sight.

I could no longer pretend that my life was normal. Not when the world was full of so much hate. And not when that hate was coming closer and closer. My eyes filled with tears. This was how Vincent saw me, I supposed. As an awful thing, less than human. I rode the rest of the way home staring straight ahead to avoid more posters telling me what I was quickly realizing: my life was not a fairy tale anymore.

And perhaps it never would be again.

CHAPTER FIVE

"You see, Rose?" Papa frowned intensely, ignoring his dinner. "This is what I've been saying since November! We're not safe here anymore. We should leave France! Now!"

I slouched in my chair, deeply regretting telling my parents what had happened with Vincent at school. I used my fork to hide some of my spinach under my dinner roll. I wished I could dig a hole and bury the entire awful day as easily.

"Max, you're overreacting," said Maman. She took a bite of her chicken and a sip of her wine. "It was just a stupid boy. We're safe here in the Free Zone."

I sat between them, unsure of which side I agreed with more. It seemed to me they were both right. Vincent *was* a stupid—if unreasonably handsome—boy, it was true. But were we safe here? I hoped so, yet I was less sure than ever before.

"There is no 'Free Zone' anymore, Rose!" insisted Papa. "We should disappear, like Rabbi Bernstein did."

Disappear? I thought with alarm. For some reason I pictured Mademoiselle Petitjean erasing the day's lesson from the blackboard. In a matter of moments, with a few bold strokes, all those words and numbers would be wiped away. Would we be like that? Gone without a trace?

With her glasses on, Maman looked smart and serious—as always. But her eyes told another story. As did her voice, which wavered as the subject of Rabbi Bernstein's mysterious disappearance came up. For years, the rabbi had been an important fixture of our community. We didn't know him well, as we weren't members of his congregation. But we often saw his wife at the market, and he and Papa were friendly. And then, one day, we heard a rumor that the Bernsteins had left town in the middle of the night, with no explanation or forwarding address.

"How can you even suggest that?" asked Maman. "Leave, without saying goodbye to our friends? What about our house, our furniture?"

"Our furniture?" Papa's eyes flashed with annoyance. "Rose, Jews are being rounded up in Marseille! How can you worry about furniture?"

Maman shook her head emphatically. She spoke to Papa like she did to me when I made a careless error on a math test or tried to go out to play with my friends before practicing piano. "Foreign Jews, Max!" she said slowly, as if to clear up his apparent confusion. "And religious Jews. That's not us. We don't even go to temple."

"Rose, are you forgetting that you were born in Antwerp and I am from Brussels?"

"I was born here," I offered. Both of them ignored me.

My mother's brow furrowed deeply. "I am a French citizen! So are you!" she practically yelled, startling me. It was not like Maman to raise her voice. "We have the papers to prove it!" she continued. "I have lived here for practically my entire life, Max. I was a little girl when my parents moved here. France is my home!"

There was a dreadful silence. Then Papa spoke quietly.

"It was Simone's home, too," he said.

My mother's face softened, for she knew what he meant. I did too—we had heard nothing from Aunt Simone and her family since the Vel' d'Hiv roundup. I still held out hope that they were okay—there were lots of reasons people might be too busy to write, or letters might be intercepted in the Occupied Zone. But their silence was troubling, at the very least.

Maman reached out and took Papa's hands in hers. "Max, darling. If we have to leave, we'll leave. I promise," she said. "But let's just wait it out for a little while longer. Things can't go on like this forever."

I nodded. This was what I wanted to believe. "Maman is right, Papa," I added. "Everything will be fine—you'll see."

"I hope so, Sara," replied Papa. His voice was so quiet, it sounded like he was praying. That was something I had never heard him do. My father was a man of science, not religion.

I took a bite of my spinach, glad Maman had won the argument. I swallowed bite after bite, wishing I had never mentioned Vincent in the first place. Spinach was not my favorite vegetable, but according to Maman it was good for me and would make me stronger. I was willing to do whatever it took to get stronger, so I could get through this difficult time. I did not want to leave France, bad as things were. I added my own silent prayer to Papa's. *Please make my life return to normal soon. All of our lives,* I added quickly. I missed my playful, joyful parents.

Maman's voice snapped me back to attention. "In the meantime, Sara," she ordered, "you stay far away from that Vincent boy. Okay?"

"Of course, Maman."

After dinner, I cleared the dishes, finished my homework, and dutifully practiced a couple of piano pieces. When I was finally done with my chores, I headed for my room and the sanctuary of my sketchbook. I was lost in that world when I heard a faint knock at my bedroom door.

"Allô?" I called in response.

The door opened and my father peered in. "Sara, it's late," he said. "You should be asleep by now."

"I know," I told him without looking up. "I'm just finishing a drawing I started in school today. Mademoiselle Petitjean says I'm a good artist," I added proudly.

"That doesn't surprise me in the least. You have a gift, Sara. But now it's time for bed."

I hesitated. I wanted to tell him that I needed to keep drawing, at least for a little while longer. Especially after what Vincent had said. I needed to take what he had made dirty and make it special and clean and mine again. Usually, the simple act of drawing carried me far away from my day-to-day worries. But I had started noticing that my fears and concerns did not always go away. They had begun patiently waiting for my pencil to stop moving, so they could swoop back in.

"Good night, Sara," he said, turning to leave.

"Wait. Papa?" I called out.

"Yes?"

The question hadn't even quite formed in my mind before the words came tumbling out of my mouth. "Why—why do they hate us, Papa? Why do people hate Jewish people?"

"Not all people, Sara," Papa corrected me. "You must never think it's all people. Only some people."

"Bad people?" I whispered, clutching my stuffed puppy, Brigitte, to my chest.

Papa sighed. He came over to my bed and sat down. "I try not to think in terms of good and bad," he said. "I prefer to think in terms of light and dark. I believe that all people have a light that shines inside of them."

"A light?" I asked.

Papa nodded earnestly. Maman had taken me to see Papa give a presentation once, at a medical college nearby. I remembered how impressed I was by his passion for his work as a surgeon. He was fascinated with all that medical interventions could do. But it was clear that what attracted him to his field was something that went even deeper—it was about saving people's lives. The tone he took in my darkened bedroom told me that he was sharing something similarly important.

"This light allows us to see into other people's hearts, to see the beauty there," he continued. "The love. The sadness. The humanity. Some people, though, have lost this light. They have darkness inside them, so that is all they see in others: darkness. No beauty. No love."

He gently brushed my hair out of my face. "Why do they hate us?" he asked. "Because they cannot see our light. Nor can they extinguish it. As long as we shine our light, we win. They will never take our light from us. Do you understand that, Sara?"

"Yes, Papa."

He smiled. "Now, I have a favor to ask."

"What is it?"

"I want you to keep wearing your winter boots to school."

I frowned, out of confusion as much as unhappiness, and hugged Brigitte even tighter. What a strange request! I couldn't help but protest.

"What? No! It's April already! I don't need my winter boots."

Maman might have argued back, using logic and reason.

Papa did not. "Please, little bird? For me?" he said.

"But why?"

"Just promise me."

It was rare for Papa to ask anything of me. So even though it was a ridiculous request, I quickly caved. "Oh, all right. Fine. I promise."

Papa seemed relieved by my answer. I said good night and snuggled down into my covers, cuddling Brigitte. I had already thought up a solution that would make everyone happy. In the morning, I would leave the house wearing my heavy winter boots to please Papa. But the second I was out of view, I'd swap them for my regular shoes.

The next morning, I headed out the door with my father.

Maman called after me for leaving without a hug, but we were in a hurry, so I ran back and gave her a quick bisou instead. "Mwah!" I cried dramatically, darting off again as fast as my dreaded boots would carry me. When we reached the main square, Papa said goodbye at the fountain before heading to his office.

"À bientôt, little bird," he said, gathering me into a quick embrace. He glanced down at my feet. "And thank you for wearing your boots."

"Of course." I smiled. "Have a nice day, Papa."

I watched as he hurried off. As soon as he turned the corner, I wriggled out of my bulky clodhoppers. From my bag I withdrew the pair of red shoes that I had practically begged Maman to buy me, back when Jews were welcome in all the local stores. I slipped them onto my feet and buckled the lovely straps, ignoring a pang of guilt.

Instantly, I felt like a princess. Sure, I was cold—but at least I looked fashionable! And with everything that's going on, I told myself, I need a little happiness. Walking into school wearing those gorgeous red shoes made everything feel a bit better. What's more, they told the world that Sara Blum was a chic girl with a good head on her shoulders, striding confidently into the future. At that moment, I very much wanted to show that side of myself to the world.

And what Papa didn't know about my shoe swap wouldn't hurt him!

CHAPTER SIX

That day was a Wednesday, so we had art class first thing in the morning. Every week, I looked forward to Wednesday. But as soon as art class came to an end, we had to return from the art room for my least favorite subject: math. It felt incredibly unfair to have my worst class immediately after my best one.

I dragged my feet every step of the way, resigned to my fate. To make matters worse, I had purposely left my sketchbook in the art room so I wouldn't be tempted to doodle.

"Let's review the Pythagorean theorem," said Mademoiselle Petitjean, standing at the board. Pointing at a formula with her chalk, she began to explain, "You'll notice that a squared plus b squared—"

"Mademoiselle Petitjean."

We all turned to see Pastor Luc, the directeur of the school, standing in the doorway of the room.

"Can I have a word with you, please?" he asked, his tone urgent.

"Yes, Pastor Luc."

He whispered in her ear. I couldn't hear his words, but I saw him looking around the room as he spoke. He locked eyes with me for a split second, his brow furrowed.

I glanced over at Mariann. Her expression told me she was getting the same feeling I was. Something was wrong.

When Pastor Luc left, Mademoiselle Petitjean turned to face us. She seemed frustrated, yet determined.

"Children, I have to leave for a few minutes," she said. "I want all of you to behave until I return, okay?"

Under normal circumstances, an opportunity like this would lead to some light classroom chaos. We weren't babies, but it was just too tempting to leave our seats and gossip with our friends. But this was clearly far from a normal time.

"Ruth? Sara?"

I looked up, surprised to hear my name called.

"Will you please get your things and come with me?" Mademoiselle Petitjean said. "Quickly," she added.

"Me! Why?" I asked, exchanging glances with Mariann and Sophie.

"Why?" echoed Ruth.

"I'll explain outside. Come, girls. Quick, quick!" She ushered us out into the hall. I heard her call back to the rest of my classmates, "The rest of you, stay in your seats until I return. Be good, children."

Taking me and Ruth by the hand, she marched us through the halls and down the stairs. Her tone was brisk and business-like. "There's a roundup of the Jews in Aubervilliers-aux-Bois," she informed us. "The Nazis are on their way here to get the children. A maquisard is going to take you and the other Jewish children to hide in the woods."

Maquisard? Roundup? Nazis? The words ran in circles as what she was saying began to register. I knew maquisards were members of the Maquis, the French underground that was resisting the Germans. The Nazis were coming here? For us?

"There he is!" cried Mademoiselle Petitjean when we reached the ground floor. "Let's hurry." Then she looked at me and her expression suddenly changed. "But, Sara, where is your coat?"

"I left it in the art room this morning," I confessed. At the time, I had assumed I would swing by to collect my sketchbook and coat before heading home. "I'm sorry," I added.

"It's okay," she said, though she looked concerned. Quickly, she untied her yellow scarf. "Here, take this," she said, looping it around my neck. "It'll keep you warm."

I was grateful for her kind gesture. And also overwhelmed. Everything was happening so fast. "I'm scared," I whispered as she pulled the scarf tightly around me.

Mademoiselle Petitjean leaned in, her face inches from mine. "I know, but you're going to be all right," she told me. "Just remember . . . you're not alone."

"Okay," I said, trying to match my tone to hers.

As we left the school, a chilly breeze made me look up. Tiny flakes of snow were falling from the sky. They landed on my bare arms and Ruth's winter coat. Other teachers joined us in the courtyard, leading their students, too. I saw Nathan, Daniel, Rebecca, Saul, and several other kids. Saul was only six and Rebecca was fifteen, and it looked like there were about twelve of us—all grades and ages. We gathered around Pastor Luc and the maquisard, who were standing under the gated archway. The maquisard was a tall, lanky young man dressed in gray and olive-drab clothing, including a gray wool cap. Over his shoulder was a long rifle, the barrel pointed at the sky.

"Children, pay close attention," Pastor Luc instructed us.

"You have to stay quiet. And run fast," the maquisard told us. "Can you run fast?"

"Yes," said a boy standing near me.

"Yes," agreed Rebecca.

"Very fast," piped up Saul. This was debatable, as he was the littlest boy, but no one argued with him. I stood silently, feeling cold but also numb. *How can this be happening?* I wanted to ask. *Don't the Nazis know our village is in the Free Zone?* With a shudder, I remembered what Papa had said: *There is no more Free Zone.*

We had no time for goodbyes. When the maquisard started running toward the woods, everyone followed him.

Everyone except me.

Instead, I stood like a statue. There was a flurry of activity as the students tried to catch up with the maquisard. Meanwhile, Pastor Luc and the teachers stood off to one side, huddled together in a hushed conversation. Keeping one eye on them, I quietly began walking backward. Silently, I slipped inside the school building, hoping no one would notice me. And as soon as I got to the staircase, I bolted up it.

I ran to the bell tower and climbed higher to the belfry. It wasn't really a conscious choice; I just wanted to get as far away as possible and hide until the threat was over. On some level I suppose I was thinking about the fact that the bell hadn't worked for years. No one ever went up to the belfry.

So many thoughts ran through my head as I sat there, hiding. I felt guilty for leaving the others. I wondered about the maquisard. Who was he? How did he know what to do and where to go? He didn't look much older than some of the students at our school. As I glanced down, my stylish red shoes caught my eye. If I ruined those gorgeous shoes by running around the woods in them, I would be devastated, and my parents would be furious with me.

I sat there, shivering, and waited for someone to come and tell me that the situation had been resolved. That there had been a misunderstanding. That the threat was over. That it was time to go home. None of these things happened.

Instead, the Nazis came.

CHAPTER SEVEN

The Nazis pulled up in a truck. Their truck was followed by another truck, this one filled with gendarmes. It was a strange sight to me. In my village, the gendarmes were our local policemen. Once, when I was little, I got separated from Maman and Papa in the market square. I did what they had always instructed me to do if such a thing ever happened: looked for a gendarme. I walked up to a man in the familiar uniform and told him I was lost. He kept me safe, helped me find my parents, and even bought me a cherry-red lollipop. From that day forward, I always felt warmly about the gendarmes.

That is, until I saw those very same men piling out of their truck and conferring with the Nazis. They were clearly working together, and their common task was obviously to round up Jews. Just like what had happened in Paris. When I saw those two trucks, my knees began to shake and I felt like I might vomit.

I knew in my heart that I was not going home. Not that day. Maybe not ever.

From my hiding place high in the bell tower, I could hear them shouting the moment they got off the trucks.

"Who is in charge? We're here on official business. We have orders to follow!"

Pastor Luc ran to meet them. I watched through a narrow window in the tower as he talked to the German soldiers. One of them seemed to be the boss. He produced a piece of paper and shoved it into Pastor Luc's face.

"This is the official list," he barked. "Bring these children here immediately."

Pastor Luc bent his head, appearing to study the list intently. Then he looked up. "I am sorry to have to tell you this, but none of these children came to school today," he said.

"Oh, please!" scoffed the soldier. "You expect me to believe that? Where are you hiding them?"

At the sound of the word "hiding," I pulled back from the window. But in a few minutes, I couldn't resist peeking out again. The soldiers were still conferring with the pastor. He was shrugging his shoulders and shaking his head. "They must have been tipped off beforehand," one of the soldiers insisted.

I held my breath. The soldier in charge swore and stomped his foot. Then he shouted angrily at the others, rounding them up to leave.

But before they could board the trucks, a voice called out from a window.

"A *maquisard* took them into the woods!"

It came from a classroom below me, so I couldn't see who

it was. But Vincent's arrogant voice was unmistakable. And his words were all the German soldiers needed to hear.

"To the woods!" shouted the leader. "To the woods!"

The soldiers ran into the woods. I had not been raised in a religious household, but if ever there was a time for prayer, this was it. I closed my eyes and wished for Ruth, Rebecca, little Saul, and all the others to run far and fast. They had a head start, after all. Hopefully, it would be enough.

It was not, and I knew it as soon as I opened my eyes and looked in the direction where everyone had run. It was still snowing, but too lightly to cover their tracks. If I could see the footprints from the bell tower, there was no way the soldiers would fail to notice them.

It did not take long for the soldiers to return with the children, many of whom were crying and all of whom were shivering in the cold. Snow did not usually fall this late in spring, so none of them were wearing boots. The maquisard was with them, led by a Nazi soldier.

The Nazi leader immediately marched over. He seized the maquisard and pulled him away from the group. Some of the soldiers followed while others guided the children to the back of one of the trucks. The boss forced the maquisard to a spot on the other side of the vehicle.

"On your knees," he ordered.

At first the maquisard stood there defiantly. He stared off into the distance as if he hadn't heard the order. With a sharp whack, the Nazi brought him to his knees.

"Vive l'humanité!" the maquisard cried. It was the first time I'd ever heard that particular slogan. "Long live humanity!"

And then a shot rang out.

He fell awkwardly to one side, landing faceup. I saw red on the front of his jacket and in the snow next to him—his blood. He lay there, not moving. The snowflakes kept falling, covering his body like a blanket.

I wanted to scream, but the sound got caught in my throat. I looked around the courtyard anxiously, waiting for someone to run over and try to help him. I listened desperately for the siren of an emergency vehicle.

No one came.

The soldiers ignored him. Instead, they turned their attention to the children, lifting them up onto the back of the truck.

"Where are you taking us?" I heard little Saul ask.

"To be with your parents. You'll see them soon."

My eyes filled with tears. I very nearly cried out in my anger and frustration. *Run! Get away! They're lying to you. They just shot a man. He's lying in the snow and they don't want you to see.*

But I didn't dare make a sound. I knew I couldn't help them. They had run and tried to get away. Yet here they were, being rounded up and taken who knew where.

And who knew what my fate would be if they realized I was missing?

Pastor Luc and some of the teachers, including Mademoiselle Petitjean, came running over to the truck. They must have seen what happened to the maquisard, but they did not attend to him. This told me that it was too late.

"Wait! Please!" cried Pastor Luc, begging the German officer in charge. "I implore you, for the love of God, let these children go."

The officer scowled at him. "I should shoot you for lying to us."

I flinched and covered my face. But this time no shot came, and I dared to look again.

"I suggest you and your teachers go back inside and mind your own business," snarled the officer.

"The children *are* our business," insisted Pastor Luc.

"Go inside, or I'll shoot one of your teachers right in front of you."

This horrible threat seemed to change things for Pastor Luc. He nodded, looking down, and tried to guide Mademoiselle Petitjean back into the school. I heard him say, "Marie, there is nothing more we can do here. Let's go inside."

Marie, he called her. There was a gentleness to his voice, like the way my papa sometimes spoke to me if I was being stubborn and he didn't want to upset me further. I looked down at her, and for the first time ever, I realized how young Mademoiselle Petitjean was. Not much older than Rebecca or Vincent. Like me, she wasn't wearing a coat. Just a bright red dress that I had admired that morning, especially since it matched my pretty red shoes. Now her outfit made me think of the maquisard's blood.

Please listen to him, I silently begged. If these soldiers thought nothing of murdering the maquisard, they were certainly capable of ending her life, too.

Yet Mademoiselle Petitjean stood her ground. "But the children—" she protested.

Pastor Luc took her by the arm. "Come inside. Now!" he said firmly.

Mademoiselle Petitjean refused. After pulling her arm free, she argued with the soldiers. "Let me go with them," she asked. "They are my students, my children. I should go with them."

Some of the soldiers laughed in her face. Their leader did not. Sternly, he replied, "I advise against it, Fräulein."

Pastor Luc tried again to convince Mademoiselle Petitjean to go back inside with him. "I can't let you do this," he begged. They went round and round, Pastor Luc pleading with her to stay and Mademoiselle Petitjean stubbornly demanding that the soldiers not take her charges out of her sight.

If any of them had looked up, they might have seen me. Because I could not take my eyes off them. I needed to know what would happen. Maybe, I desperately hoped, the Nazis would just give up and let the children stay. After all, Mademoiselle Petitjean was insistent: the children couldn't go anywhere without her.

And in the end, she got her way . . . sort of. They could not stop her from being with her students. So they took her onto the truck with them. And I watched, silently, from high above, as the truck drove away.

"Then what happened?" asked Julian.

Grandmère opened her mouth to answer, only to discover that she could not speak. She took a sip of water and tried again. "Years later, my friend Ruth told me where the truck went. The children were taken to the camp at Beaune-la-Rolande. But it was too crowded there, so they were marched through the countryside to Pithiviers, about twenty kilometers—that is, twelve or thirteen miles—away. Saul and some of the other young children could not keep up with the group. Mademoiselle Petitjean stayed behind with them."

Grandmère closed her eyes but was unable to shut out the image of her teacher's face as the truck pulled away. With one arm protectively around little Saul's shoulders and the other around Ruth, she projected strength and confidence. Looking back, Grandmère remembered how strong her teacher was able to be for the children. And she wondered what Mademoiselle Petitjean had actually felt in that moment.

"And then?" Julian's voice broke the silence.

Even before Grandmère opened her eyes, she could tell that Julian was hoping for reassurance. She wanted to provide it, but it wouldn't be the truth.

"The snow kept falling. Night came," she said. "Perhaps they lost their way in the woods. Or perhaps the Nazis did not want stragglers." She shrugged sadly. "Either way, those little children never arrived in Pithiviers. In fact, Ruth was the only student that survived."

"But what about your teacher?" asked Julian.

"I don't know," Grandmère admitted. "Whatever happened to those poor little children happened to her, too. No one ever saw her again."

CHAPTER EIGHT

My red shoes. My stupid red shoes! I hugged my knees and looked down at them. How could I have fretted about something as frivolous as shoes when the world held real problems to worry about?

A man was lying dead in the snow. My classmates had been taken away in a truck by armed soldiers. And poor Mademoiselle Petitjean was with them, without a coat or even a scarf. I buried my face in it, feeling horribly guilty. She was out there in the cold, on the back of an open truck. She certainly needed her scarf more than I did.

But mostly I was thinking about Maman and Papa. Had they been taken? Where were they now? Were they safe? If they were hiding, how would I find them?

At that moment, I realized that I could hear voices. I peeked out and saw that the *gendarmes* were still in the courtyard. They had stayed behind for some reason. They were gathered around, scrutinizing a piece of paper.

"There were fifteen names on the list but only twelve children," said one of them.

Oh, mon Dieu. They were trying to locate the children who had not gotten on the truck—like me!

"They're hiding," said another gendarme. He seemed to be in charge of the others. "Go find them!" he ordered.

It was just a matter of time before they would find me. But what could I do? Where could I possibly go? The temptation to run home was strong. But even if I could do so without being seen, which seemed impossible, what would I find there? An empty house, with no sign of my parents? Or worse, Nazi soldiers sitting around our kitchen table, waiting to pounce on me?

I sat there, trying to think of a plan but falling deeper and deeper into despair. Why had I been so stupid? If I hadn't been so vain about my red shoes, I might be with Mademoiselle Petitjean and the others. That seemed like a much better choice than sitting in the belfry like a mouse in a trap.

Just then I heard footsteps on the stairs.

Perfect, I thought. Not only am I trapped like a mouse, but the cat is arriving to finish me off.

I watched the door slowly open. My heart was beating wildly. I closed my eyes, too afraid to look.

"Sara?"

I opened my eyes. And blinked repeatedly at this . . . apparition.

"They will find you here," said Tourteau, who was standing in the doorway. "But I know a way out."

I was too astonished to speak. He was the last person I

expected to see, for so many reasons. I was fairly certain no one had seen me sneak back inside. Also, we were several flights of stairs up, at the highest point of the school. I would not have thought he could navigate so many stairs on his crutches. And he was offering to help me, which would obviously put him at great risk as well. Not to mention that I had never said more than two words to this boy, despite having sat next to him for years.

"Come on!" he urged. "Follow me!"

I did not ask where we were going. I just followed him.

As we went down the stairs, we could hear the *gendarmes* yelling.

"I got one!"

"Let me go!" cried a panicked voice that clearly belonged to my friend Rachel, who was a year older than I was. I hesitated, wanting to run to her and help fight off her captors. But the urgency of Tourteau's hasty and awkward descent of the stairs, which threatened to turn into free fall at any moment, kept my focus on him.

Rachel's screams echoed in my ears as we continued down flight after flight of stairs. I tried to shut out her pitiful cries as I followed Tourteau through the crypt beneath our school's chapel, and lower still to the cellar. When we finally ran out of stairs, I tried to look around. The cellar was cold, clammy, and dark. And on top of all that, there was something else that was off-putting.

"I'm sorry," said Tourteau. In the dim light I saw him wrinkle his nose in a way that probably mirrored my own expression. He cringed, looking embarrassed. "I know it smells. But this was the only way out I could think of."

"Way . . . out?" I asked.

Tourteau nodded, gesturing down a long hallway. "Through the sewer system. It connects everything, underground."

I followed him silently, and after some time we arrived at a passage. It was so narrow, we had to walk sideways to get through. Next, we stepped down and there we were: in the sewers. Literally, knee-deep in refuse. So much for my pretty red shoes! But taking them off was inconceivable. Everything that had happened had firmly shifted my concerns from style to survival.

"Won't they find us here?" I asked nervously.

"Not if we hurry. At least, I hope not." He began to hobble determinedly through the dark tunnel. For once, I was the slow one, holding back. The sewer water was dark and murky, with an oily slick surface that glimmered in the dwindling light. All around, I heard pipes dripping and echoing hauntingly.

Tourteau turned to see what was keeping me. I must have looked like a fool, shuffling and splashing my way along, glancing around in fear that some kind of subterranean sea monster would rear up and bite me.

"You must be freezing," he said.

"No," I protested. "I'm f-f-fine."

"Here." He took off his coat and held it out to me. It reminded me of the day before, when he had returned my sketchbook and my friends had whispered and laughed right in front of him. Even though I was terribly cold, I knew I didn't deserve his kindness or his coat. Yet I didn't know how to explain how awful I felt.

"B-b-but . . . you will be cold," I said instead.

"I'll be all right," he replied, tipping his cap politely. "I have my hat to keep me warm. Now come on—let's go."

He continued ahead of me, carefully plodding on his crutches through the dark, churning canal of filth. I had no choice but to scramble to stay on my feet and to keep up. The water was so frigid! I could barely feel my toes. I wrapped Tourteau's coat tightly around me, grateful to have it. I tried to think of something to say to thank him for being so selfless. I watched his back as he led the way through the tunnels. He was very thin, and I had always assumed he was weak. It had never occurred to me that all those years of using his crutches had given him a different kind of strength.

We walked for hours.

I don't know how he did it. I was so exhausted, I felt tempted to drop to my knees and cry. I can't imagine how tiring it must have been for him. But he never slowed down. And that helped, because I told myself that as long as he kept moving, so would I.

There were some lights in the tunnels, but no signs to speak of. And yet whenever we reached a turn or a crossroads, he seemed to know which way to go. Finally, after a long silence, I called out to ask something I had been wondering from the start.

"How do you know where we are?"

"I've been down here before," he told me, "helping my father with his work. Up ahead there's a tunnel that leads to the storm drains. We can take that all the way to Dannevilliers, where I live."

Dannevilliers? I imagined what I might have done, the day before, if someone had suggested a visit to Dannevilliers. I would have made a face or worse. But no one would have ever suggested such a thing in the first place. Dannevilliers was the butt of my friends' and my jokes, even though I'd never been there—and if Mariann and Sophie had, they'd never have admitted it. It was a tiny village about fifteen kilometers from my town. It had shops, like Aubervilliers-aux-Bois, but everyone said the goods sold there were cheaper and shoddier. Like many of our neighbors, Maman and Papa avoided this town because of its infamous smell. According to them, the sewers from Paris drained onto the farmland there. When I went grocery shopping with Maman, she would often admire a vendor's shiny red apples and ask where they were grown. If the answer was "Dannevilliers, madame!" she would reply politely, yet we would somehow end up purchasing our fruit from a different vendor.

"I was hoping for one of those pretty apples," I confessed on the way home after one such incident.

She made a face. "They might be nice to look at, but their taste won't be so sweet." She and Papa claimed anything grown in Dannevilliers tasted like sewage, and I of course took their word for it.

"Is something wrong?" asked Tourteau.

I shook my head. I was in no position to take issue with our destination, no matter how wretched it might smell. Besides, I was used to the smell of the sewers already.

We plodded along. It was getting dark by the time we arrived. A slim column of waning light reached us where we stood at the stairs up to the ground-level exit. I stayed below while Tourteau climbed out and checked to make sure no one was around. He returned quickly and called down.

"The coast is clear."

I climbed up to join him on the street. My dress had absorbed so much raw sewage, it felt like it weighed a thousand pounds. I couldn't feel my calves or feet. And despite having Tourteau's coat, I was shaking from the cold.

"My house is at the end of this road," said Tourteau.

I was relieved to be out of the sewers and on dry land again. The chill wind made every step painful, but I was determined to keep moving. I'd come this far—it would be terrible to collapse now. I willed my legs to just keep moving. I began counting my steps in a desperate attempt to have something to focus on. Forty-eight . . . forty-nine . . . fifty . . . fifty-one . . .

We walked to the outskirts of the village, Tourteau leading the way through back alleys and tiny one-way streets. I figured he was probably trying to avoid the main road, which made sense.

He was talking to me the whole way. I wondered if he had been talking to me in the sewers, too, and I just couldn't hear anything over the water and pipe noises. "Unfortunately, you won't be able to come inside my house," he said. "We have crazy old neighbors who are very nosy. We think they're Nazi collaborators. It's too risky."

I felt nausea rising in my throat. Nazi collaborators in tiny, run-down Dannevilliers? Was there anywhere in this world that was safe anymore?

Tourteau glanced at me. I must have looked terrified, because he began talking faster, trying to reassure me. "But there's a barn across the field. It has a hayloft. You'll be safe there for the night. After we get you settled in, I'll bring you some soup and blankets. Oh, and dry clothes. Your feet must be frozen in those shoes!"

"Yeah, they are," I admitted, deeply regretting my choice. "I should have worn my . . ."

I could not finish my sentence. If only I had worn my boots, like I'd told Papa I would. And now who knew if I would ever have the chance to apologize to him for breaking my promise? Who knew if I would even see him again?

Tourteau held me back at the edge of a house. He leaned on his crutches and peeked around it, gesturing for me to look while pointing to a dark shape on the horizon. "There's the barn. See it? But let's wait till my neighbors turn off their lights. Then it'll be safe to cross the field."

We waited silently as clouds slid over the moon. My stomach ached from hunger, and I had to hold my jaw to keep my teeth from chattering too loudly. Finally, we slipped across the road and into the tall grass of a field separating us from the barn.

"Watch your step," called Tourteau, pointing out hidden

holes and grass-covered rocks. He seemed to know every inch of the field by heart. Meanwhile, I stumbled more on my two supposedly functional legs than he did on his crutches.

"I can't see a thing," I muttered as I banged into yet another disguised boulder. I probably should have slowed down, but I was in such a hurry to get inside, where I hoped I would finally warm up. And where I hoped I might finally be able to stop running.

CHAPTER NINE

"You'll be safe in here," said Tourteau.

"Really?" I asked, looking around.

It probably sounded rude, and that wasn't my intention. But the barn we were standing in was a crumbling old disaster of a building, in terrible disrepair. It was for the best that it was dark out, so I did not get a good look at the outside of the barn when we arrived. I might have been too scared to enter if I had! But now that we were inside, I could see that there were cobwebs everywhere. And I could hear mice scurrying to move out of the way, too. When Tourteau used the word "safe," I wasn't thinking about Nazis. I was worrying about the roof of the barn collapsing and flattening me, with the walls falling down soon after, like a house of cards.

"Really," Tourteau assured me. "See the hayloft up there?" He pointed above our heads. Inside the barn, it should have been pitch black. But there were holes and gaping spots in the roof, walls, and boarded-up windows that let some slivers of moonlight in. "That's where you can hide."

I tentatively stepped out into the barn's main open space. I could see dark shapes in all directions. Many were clearly bales of hay, stacked and abandoned. There also appeared to be a broken-down, rusty old car. Some of its tires were flat and others were missing entirely. Then I looked up and realized something else was missing.

"I can't get up there," I said. "There's no ladder."

A look of panic crossed Tourteau's face, followed by one of inspiration. He set aside his crutches and carefully kneeled down.

"I can't . . . step on you," I said, horrified.

"It's fine," he insisted. "I'm strong, really. I'll help you up and you can pull me up after."

I glanced around in the dark, trying to find another option. But there was nothing I could see, so finally I took a deep breath and gingerly put my foot on his shoulder. He was right—like I saw in the sewers, his upper body strength was impressive, and my weight didn't seem to faze him in the least. I reached up, grabbed the edge of the loft, and pulled myself up the rest of the way.

In the hayloft, I kneeled and peered down. Finding Tourteau's hands in the dark, I accepted his crutches, then pulled him up to join me. Despite his strength, he was light, so I was able to do it easily.

"You'll be safe up here for tonight," he told me. "Cover yourself with the hay. It will keep you warm." He showed me how to gather it. "I used to play up here when I was little, before I got polio." He looked around, smiling for the first time since our journey began. The barn, as spooky and unfamiliar as it was to me, seemed to be a comforting place for him. "Don't worry," he added, "you'll get used to the smell."

It did smell, but it wasn't really a bad smell. Certainly not the kind of smell I had always imagined would exist in Dannevilliers. It smelled like hay, and like cows or horses, though the cobwebs suggested that livestock hadn't been kept in the barn for quite some time. I was going to tell him that it didn't smell that bad, but an odd chirping noise and some shuffling above our heads distracted me.

"What is that sound, coming from over there?" I asked, pointing up and toward the far corner.

"Oh, those are just the bats roosting in the rafters. If you leave them alone, they'll leave you alone. Otherwise, it's a great place, right?"

"Huh?" I looked at him, confused.

"That was actually a little joke."

"Ohh!" I said, surprised. Then it hit me. It was funny.

"Ha." A nervous little laugh escaped my lips. Then the absurdity of my day suddenly struck me. If a fortune-teller had magically appeared in art class that morning and told me that by the end of the day I would be sitting in a hayloft in Dannevilliers laughing at a joke told by Tourteau, I would have advised her to find a new job.

"Ha-ha-ha-ha! Hahahahaha!" Something inside me broke loose and I began to laugh for real.

"Ha-ha-ha! Hahahaha!" Tourteau joined me, clearly pleased at having made me laugh.

"Hahahaha! Ha-ha-ha-ha-ha!" It felt so good. I laughed so hard, it was difficult to stop.

"Hee-hee-hee!"

I hadn't laughed like that in a long time. Certainly not since all the trouble began. I remembered that awful day at the ice cream shop. It seemed like a million years ago, and yet it felt like if you lined up all the days between that day and this one, there was a sort of domino effect. One little thing toppling over into the next and the next until the moment when Pastor Luc interrupted our math class and everything changed.

I wiped away my tears of laughter, my emotions suddenly shifting. I almost couldn't bring myself to say what I was wondering. And yet I couldn't not ask.

With a quavering voice, I asked, "Did you see what they did to the maquisard?"

"Yes," said Tourteau simply. His furrowed brow told me it had upset him as much as it had me. "But let's not think about that now," he suggested.

I felt a flash of concern. I knew he was trying to help, but his words made me remember that there were other things we shouldn't think about. What could be worse than what they had done to the maquisard? The unimaginable answer came rushing at me.

"But what if something happened to my parents?" I asked.

"Your parents are fine. They're probably hiding, just like you." Tourteau's voice was confident, as if he had just settled them into the hayloft of a barn down the road. "Speaking of parents, though, I should go tell mine what's going on."

"Wait. Are you sure?" I asked. I had never met Tourteau's parents. I knew his father was a sewer worker, but that was about all I knew.

As if he could read my mind, he nodded. "Don't worry. You can trust my parents, just like you can trust me."

Could I trust him? I was beginning to wonder if I could trust anyone. The sympathies of someone like Vincent were obvious. But what about all the other students? Did they stay in their seats obediently, with no thoughts of what might be going on in the courtyard? And what about the teachers? I didn't know what to believe about them, but I knew in my heart I could trust someone like Mademoiselle Petitjean, who was willing to get on a truck to protect her students. And I knew I could also trust Tourteau.

It suddenly occurred to me that after all he'd done for me, I had done very little to express my appreciation. My voice cracked as I stumbled over my words.

"I . . . I don't know how to thank you, Tourteau. You saved my life."

"Oh, it's okay." He seemed flustered, and perhaps even a little embarrassed, by my outpouring. "Though I do have one suggestion . . . ," he added.

"Yes. Anything!" I replied gratefully.

"Well, maybe you can call me by my real name instead of Tourteau?"

The request took me by surprise. Now it was my turn to be embarrassed, and more than a little. Obviously, his real name was not Tourteau! It was . . . oh, dear, what was it?

"Yes! Of course! Umm . . . umm . . . ," I stammered, trying to come up with it.

"My name is Julien. Julien Beaumier."

He extended his hand, as if we were meeting for the first time. And in a way, we were. He was no longer Tourteau, the boy I had, at best, ignored and, at worst, treated as no better than a sewer rat. The boy whose face I never paid any attention to, instead seeing only his awkward gait and his omnipresent crutches. The boy who had risked his life to help me escape.

I took his hand in mine and gave it a formal shake.

"Julien," I repeated.

"Julian?" said Julian incredulously. "Like . . . my name?"

"Mais oui," his grandmother told him. "His family used the traditional French spelling: J-U-L-I-E-N. That is the name, of all the names in the world, that I have held closest to my heart. It is the name I gave to your father. And it is the name he gave to you. Julian."

"Wow. I mean, I guess that makes sense. After what he did for you."

Grandmère nodded solemnly. My dear boy, she said to herself, you have no idea.

CHAPTER TEN

After Tourteau—or rather, Julien—left the barn, I tried to make my eyes adjust to the dim light. But it was no use. I was so physically and emotionally drained that straining my eyes to look around me proved to be too much. My stomach rumbled and ached, and it dawned on me that I hadn't had anything to eat or drink all day.

I wrapped myself in hay, like Julien had showed me, and closed my eyes. I kept my ears focused, questioning every whisper of the wind through the many cracks in the walls. What if the Nazis tracked us here and were about to close in on me?

"Please come back, please come back, please come back," I chanted to myself through chattering teeth.

A short while later, I heard noises coming from below me. My eyes flew open, but when I saw the glint of light from a lantern, the rest of me remained paralyzed by fear. I was sure that the Nazis had found me. I braced myself, knowing the next voice I heard would be that of the horrible German soldier who shot the *maquisard*.

It would probably be the last sound I ever heard.

"Sara? It's me."

I quickly dug myself out of my hay pile and scrambled over to the edge of the loft. Julien's voice gave me the tiny burst of hope I needed, and seeing him standing, flanked by his parents, in the light of a lantern he was holding, added to my joy.

Julien's father helped me down from the loft. I was grateful that he did. I was so exhausted, I might have slipped and fallen if I had tried to do it alone.

"Don't worry, chérie," Julien's mother said to me. "You are safe here."

Julien's father nodded. "Julien told us everything that has happened. We will take care of you until we can find your parents." Then he and Julien's mother wrapped a warm orange blanket around me. I pulled it close to me and noticed that it smelled like lavender. She handed me a parcel, which turned out to contain several warm, dry articles of clothing.

"I am Vivienne, and this is Jean-Paul," said Julien's mother. "You must be famished, chérie. Why don't you get out of your wet things? Then you can have some soup while we clean the place up for you." She wore a dark green dress with buttons up the front, and a cardigan sweater the color of Dijon mustard. She was nowhere near as beautiful as Maman—no one was, in my opinion—but she had a kind face and a forthright manner that set me at ease almost immediately. Jean-Paul was tall and serious-looking, with a mustache like Papa's, only thicker. He wore a workman's cap, similar to the one Julien often wore, and I noticed that his pants were tucked into his work boots—presumably to keep them dry in the sewers.

I ducked into a corner of the barn, and they all turned away while I quickly shed my soaked garments and sopping shoes. The clothes Vivienne provided were loose and ill-fitting, for which she apologized when I emerged wearing them. "As soon as your things are clean and dry, I will return them to you," she promised.

"But now that you're changed, you should eat," suggested Julien. "My mother is an excellent cook. Her *potage* is one of my favorite soups. All the vegetables come from our garden."

I accepted the steaming bowl from Vivienne and began to eat heartily, forgoing any attempt at the manners Maman had tried to instill in me. It was thick and savory, with potatoes and herbs, and I quickly polished it off. It made me think of the chicken soup that Maman would often make, rich with potatoes, onions, carrots, and dill. I felt an intense wave of longing for her. I wanted to run into her arms. I wanted to feel her hug me tight, like she'd never let go. And I wanted to tell her something.

I pictured myself pulling back from that hug and gazing up at her. *You're wrong, Maman*, I would say. *Nothing in Dannevilliers tastes like the sewers.* I imagined she would laugh and draw me close again.

Yet that happy thought quickly led to a sudden realization. The flavor of produce grown in Dannevilliers wasn't the only thing Maman had been wrong about.

Maman might have won the argument about staying in France longer.

But Papa had been right.

After I finished my soup, I noticed that the Beaumier family was looking around the loft and quietly conferring. Jean-Paul was pointing and Julien was nodding. Vivienne went over to the corner and came back with a broom.

"What's going on?" I asked.

"Well, it's possible you'll be here with us for a while," answered Julien. "So we'd like to make your accommodations a little more, shall we say, livable."

"That's not necessary," I protested, my manners having been minorly restored by the nourishment.

Julien held up a hand. "We insist. It would be terrible to have you escape from the Nazis only to catch your death of hay fever. Or spider bites!"

"At least let me help," I offered. I put down my bowl and stumbled to my feet.

"Oh no no," replied Vivienne. "I won't hear of it! After all you've been through."

"But . . . I want to be useful. Just give me a job."

Vivienne smiled. Using her broom, she gently "swept" me over to a spot she had cleared on the barn floor. "You can sit here and watch us work. Your job is to tell us if we miss anything. Okay?" Her tone suggested that this was not an actual question. So I did as I was told and sat.

For the next few hours, I dutifully watched as they

cleaned out the dust and cobwebs and swept the floor. Jean-Paul climbed up to the hayloft and created a wall out of the hay bales, lined up with the front edge of the loft. That created the illusion that the loft was fully stocked. Anyone who came into the barn would look up and quickly conclude that the hayloft could not possibly contain anything other than hay.

"It's perfect," cried Julien, checking his father's work from below. "I can't see anything from down here."

It was a great plan, from what I could tell. You would never guess anyone was up there. From my assigned spot, next to a barrel on the barn floor, I gazed up with gratitude. I looked forward to climbing back up as soon as they finished cleaning, and finding what they had promised would await me on the other side of the hay wall: a tidy room created just for me.

But the Beaumiers weren't quite finished. They were a hardworking trio, and they were clearly determined to see this project through. So I sat and waited as patiently as I could. After a while, I lay down and rested my eyes. Soon the soft rhythmic whisk-whisk-whisk of Vivienne's broom turned into a soft fluttering by my ear. A little white bird was sitting on my shoulder. It gently tugged on my hair and trilled softly, inviting me to join it and take flight.

So I did.

I spread my wings and felt a current of air lift me higher and higher. I flew away from Dannevilliers, flying over Aubervilliers-aux-Bois, and the mountains, and the bluebell glade of the Mernuit. As high as I was, I recognized all these sights easily: the bell tower of my school, the town square, the glowing purple blossoms of the forest floor. I followed the moon to distant cities, over train stations and railway tracks.

I flew very, very far, though I felt no tiredness and no pain. What I felt was an urgency to get to where I was going. Although I wasn't sure where that was until I saw her.

Maman.

I circled above, watching her. She was wearing her long yellow coat, which I had dubbed her "kittycat coat" when I was little. The name had stuck. She hadn't worn it in ages, but it was always my favorite because the fabric around the collar was as soft as a newborn kitten's fur. She was standing outside a long, low brick-red building with a tall tower at the center. The moon was up behind the building, since it was nighttime. But I didn't wonder where she was going so late in the evening, or why she was wearing that coat.

At that moment, she turned and looked up. Somehow, she saw me.

"Sara," she said, because she knew it was me.

"That's right, Maman," I said. "I'm here. And I'm going to be okay. And so are you." Only she couldn't understand me, because I was a bird. Yet I could tell it made her happy to know that I was safe.

"Sara."

"Sara?"

"Huh?"

"I'm so sorry to wake you, Sara, but I'm leaving now."

Vivienne was on her knees, gazing at me with concern. "Jean-Paul and Julien already left. I will come back with more food and water tomorrow. All right, chérie?"

I sat up slowly, as the room swam into view and I realized I had drifted off. It took me a moment to sort out what was real and what had been a dream. And another moment to find my words. "Yes. Thank you," I finally said.

"I'll help you back up to the loft, but you'll need to hide yourself—Jean-Paul left you a passageway so you can slide in and out between the hay bales. Once you're up there, please don't come down from the loft for any reason."

"What about—" I asked, feeling embarrassed.

"We set things up for you, up there," said Vivienne. "It's a bucket, which is not ideal, obviously. But I'll help take care of things—you'll see." She sighed. "And there's really no other option. Julien explained about our neighbors, yes? They don't usually come to the barn, but still, let's be safe."

I nodded. "Yes. I won't go down."

Vivienne seemed reassured by my words. And honestly, I meant what I said. The girl who had swapped her practical boots for her frivolous red shoes was someone I no longer recognized.

I must have looked sad, for Vivienne's face softened even further. "I know this is hard, chérie, but stay strong," she urged, cupping her hands around my face and looking deep into my eyes. "You will be with your maman and papa soon. Until that day comes, we will take good care of you, I promise."

It was only when she hugged me that I started to cry. I had not cried all day, but once the tears came, I could not stop them.

"Oh, you poor thing," said Vivienne, holding me tighter and cradling my head tenderly. "There, there. It's going to be okay. You'll see."

I only cried harder.

Her embrace was so warm, yet I felt like I would never be warm again.

Her arms reminded me of my maman's arms, and the way it felt when she wrapped them around me. Her never-let-you-go hugs.

I cried, too, because in my heart I knew that I would never feel my maman's arms around me again. I knew, from my dream, that I would never see my beautiful maman again.

"But you did, Grandmère," said Julian hopefully, "didn't you?"

His grandmother didn't answer at first. Why, after all these years, were the words so hard? She could picture her mother in her mind's eye, just as she had in the dream. And she felt a tug at her heart, even after so many years. It made no sense—it was so long ago and she had been a mere child. Yet she always felt a pang of guilt when she thought of her mother, as if there was something she had neglected to do for her. Ridiculous that after all this time, her brain was stuck in its childish mode when it came to such things.

"I learned what happened much later," she finally told Julian. "That morning, when my father made me wear my boots, I kissed her goodbye and headed off to the square with him. We were in a hurry, so I didn't even hug her. Later that day, the Gestapo came for her. They put her on a train to Drancy, just outside Paris. And from there, they transported her to Auschwitz."

She took a deep breath before continuing.

"That is where she died."

PART TWO

I hear your cries, you little voices of children. . . .
—Muriel Rukeyser, "Seventh Elegy: The Dream-Singing Elegy"

"The next few days and nights were the hardest of my life," Grandmère told Julian. "I was so scared that the Nazis would find me. I worried about my parents and missed them desperately. And I struggled with the lack of clarity about, well, everything. How long would I have to hide in the hayloft? How would we know it was safe to venture out? And if I could leave—where would I go, and how would I reunite with my parents?"

"How old were you?" asked Julian.

"I was more or less your age. Just about thirteen."

"And this was pre-internet, obviously. Right?"

"Correct," Grandmère replied with a little chuckle.

"I didn't mean for playing games and streaming videos," Julian quickly added. "I just meant you couldn't use the internet to look for your parents. Because it's really good for that kind of stuff. Like, this one time, our neighbors' Yorkie, Chewie, got out. They put it online and someone found him within a few hours." He suddenly looked worried. "I'm sorry—I wasn't comparing you to a lost dog, Grandmère."

"I know, mon cher. I know."

"So what did you do?"

"What could I do?" Grandmère shrugged. "I was stuck in the hayloft, unable to show my face. I relied on the Beaumiers, who could come and go, and who were determined to find my parents. I'm not sure how they were able to feed me, since food was strictly rationed at the time. But each day they would bring something for me to eat, and—if I was lucky—news."

CHAPTER ONE
Spring 1943

"Sara? You awake? It's me, Vivienne."

Every time I heard a noise, I would freeze. I'm not sure if the Beaumiers knew that, but they always made a point of identifying themselves when they entered the barn. The wall of hay that Jean-Paul had constructed served its purpose, keeping my little room out of view, but there was a spot I could slide through by turning sideways to help my visitors climb up. I also used this slim doorway as an extra window, to peer down and imagine how luxurious it might be if I could simply descend and explore the barn a little.

At the sound of Vivienne's voice, I peeked out.

"Bonjour, ma petite," she said in greeting, holding up two market sacks.

"Bonjour, Madame Beaumier," I replied politely.

She hesitated, looking mildly uncomfortable. Realizing my mistake, I tried again. "Bonjour, Vivienne."

The corners of her mouth curled up immediately. "That's more like it."

I leaned down and accepted her parcels so she could climb up and join me. Under cover of darkness, the Beaumiers had quietly moved a few pieces of furniture into the hayloft for me. The lavender-scented blanket was now spread across a simple hay mattress. A small selection of books was arranged in a few carefully stacked potato crates. Vivienne directed me to set her bags down on an old wooden table they had hoisted into the hayloft a few nights earlier. She joined me at it, sitting in one of the two mismatched chairs.

"Any news?" I asked as she began pulling items from the bags. Each day there would be food and a few more things to make my space homier. Today she had brought half a loaf of crusty bread, a wedge of cheese, and some apples. I gratefully accepted these items, though my hunger to hear about my parents was actually what gnawed at me the most.

Vivienne pulled out a book and a pair of tin plates. She set these items down and sadly shook her head. "I'm sorry, Sara. I wish I could tell you something—anything!—but I am afraid I can't today. I've asked everyone I can think of. As you know, there are many people I cannot ask, for fear of having them discover our secret."

"Of course," I replied, remembering what Julien had told me about their next-door neighbors, the Nazi collaborators. "Thank you for everything," I added, trying not to sound too despondent.

"I only wish we could do more," said Vivienne, patting my arm. "Jean-Paul is trying to make arrangements for your safe transport. We had hoped he could convince some friends to take you with them across the border to Switzerland. Their plan is to leave as soon as possible. Unfortunately, it doesn't look like that plan will work."

"Why not?"

Vivienne sighed. "The Germans have opened a new headquarters—they call it a Kommandantur—in Dannevilliers. Before, we would hear about them marching and setting up their strongholds in the cities. It all seemed so far away. But now they're here, and there are Nazis everywhere."

She got up from the table and went over to a boarded-up window, where tiny beams of light broke through gaps between the boards. She leaned forward and looked out, taking in my only view of the world outside.

"I suppose it's a good thing that you can't see much from here," she finally said. "But take my word for it. Every road in and out of the village is heavily guarded. Even if we could get you to our friends' home without being detected, their car is sure to be searched when they try to leave. It's simply not worth the risk, because if they find you . . ." Her voice trailed off.

"What?" I asked.

She forced a smile. "We're just not going to let that happen." Then she asked brightly, "Would now be a good time to attend to your hygiene?"

"Yes, please." This was quickly becoming a ritual of ours. Each day, she would remove my bucket, clean it out, and return it. If this was disturbing or even disgusting to her, she never showed any sign of it.

Once a week, she would also bring up an extra pitcher of

fresh water. Then I would sit on the floor and lean back against a chair while she washed my hair in a basin she had provided for this purpose. The water was never particularly warm, as it came from a hose, but I was grateful nonetheless. Those moments, feeling her hands gently caressing my scalp, were some of my most peaceful ones in the hayloft.

"Vivienne?" I asked, closing my eyes to keep the soap out.

"Hmm?"

"Is there any way you could sneak me into your house?"

Vivienne was silent for a moment. I opened my eyes, fearing that I had offended her in some way. The last thing I wanted was to seem unappreciative, after they had so kindly made a hiding place for me. But I couldn't help wishing I could be in a real house, for so many reasons. In a real house, other people would be around, so I wouldn't have to jump at the slightest sound. In a real house, the walls wouldn't have gaps and holes that let the chill winds find me. In a real house, I could use a real toilet, wash myself from a faucet, sit in a comfortable chair. . . .

But it was immediately clear from her face that if I felt bad for asking, she felt worse for not being able to say yes.

"I'm so sorry," said Vivienne. "I wish it didn't have to be this way. But our neighbors, the Lafleurs . . ." She shook her head. "We just can't trust them. It's horrible to say, but I think it's true: The Nazis have gotten to them. And now they are spies."

"How do you know?" I asked.

Vivienne poured a little more water on my hair and resumed her massaging. "I suppose you could call it a woman's intuition. The funny thing is we used to be friends, Madame Lafleur and I. That is, we weren't close friends, but we were neighbors and we got along and helped each other. Our house is part of the same building, you see. If you were facing it, we would be on the left and they would be on the right."

I closed my eyes again, picturing a tidy brick house—not fancy but well maintained, with different-colored shutters for each side. Let's see . . . I would make the Beaumiers' side have cheerful yellow shutters and a matching front door, in the same shade as Mademoiselle Petitjean's scarf. And the Lafleurs would have light blue shutters and a matching door. I imagined a man and a woman standing at the second-floor window. In my mind, they didn't look like spies. But what did spies look like? Wasn't the point that they could be anyone . . . even a married couple living in a tiny town in the middle of nowhere?

"The Lafleurs are a good bit older than us, so Jean-Paul and I went out of our way to check in on them and be of assistance when they needed it. When Madame Lafleur started using a cane, I noticed and made a habit of picking up some things for her when I went to the market."

"That was nice of you," I said. I adjusted my mental picture accordingly, adding a cane and gray hair to the woman and thinning hair to the man.

"It was not a big deal," replied Vivienne. "And she seemed to appreciate it, so I kept doing it. I was going anyway, and it was easy for me to pick up their milk and other items. But as time went on, things changed. That is, they changed. They stopped speaking to me. To any of us. They keep to themselves and almost never go out. They just sit at their front window all day like a couple of sentries. It's sad, really."

Again the image in my head shifted. Now the older couple seemed sinister. They were still at the window, but they were whispering and frowning. The man looked down at Vivienne, pointing as she went out her front door. The woman furrowed her brow and nodded. Clearly, they were of the belief that the Beaumiers were up to no good.

"All set," said Vivienne, wrapping a towel around my hair. I got to my feet awkwardly and plunked myself into the free chair while Vivienne poured the gray sudsy water from my hair-washing basin into my toilet bucket.

"So you stopped bringing them things?" I asked.

Vivienne gave a little laugh. "I probably should. But I told myself that whatever their problem is, I won't let it become mine. I still bring them their milk each day and leave it on their front step, and they take it inside without a word. And now that you're here, I feel like it would seem odd to stop delivering it. The last thing I want to do is change my routine in any way that might give them a reason to be suspicious of us."

"That makes sense," I admitted.

"No," said Vivienne. "None of this makes sense. But I have come to accept that certain battles are not worth fighting, even if one is right. That is why I will keep smiling at the Lafleurs. I will do everything in my power to keep them from seeing you."

I knew she was doing the right thing. But I couldn't help feeling frustrated and angry. I wanted to confront those awful Lafleurs and yell at them. *How can you hate me and want to send* people like me away? I would say. You don't even know me! I'm just a kid! The thought of running out the door, feeling the sunshine on my face, and yelling those words at the Lafleurs' frowning faces made my heart race with excitement.

And terror.

I could do no such thing. I couldn't run. I couldn't yell. I couldn't even leave the barn.

All I could do was wait, and pray for the war to end.

I spent a lot of time waiting. Waiting for darkness, which felt less safe in some ways but safer in others. Waiting for often-elusive sleep to come, while staring up at the barn roof . . . or rather, staring at the holes in the roof. Waiting for Vivienne to appear, as she did daily. This was especially hard when I was hungry, or my bucket began to smell particularly pungent. Or both, which was frequently the case.

One day, it seemed to me that Vivienne might be running late. I had no clock, so I couldn't tell for sure. But the sun appeared to be higher in the sky, and I felt hungrier than usual. I had begun doing some daily exercises to keep my body strong, so I told myself that perhaps that was the reason for my increased appetite. But with each passing minute my worries grew. Had the Lafleurs turned her in? Had she been detained? Were the Nazis on their way to put a swift end to my stay in the barn?

"Sara? Allô? C'est moi!"

I felt a wave of relief. Quickly, I dashed over to the hayloft's edge.

"Bonjour, Mada—" I caught myself. "Bonjour, Vivienne!"

She beamed happily. Her smile lit up the gloomy space.

"Bonjour, ma petite!" she called. "Here, can you take these?" She handed me her bags, and within moments she was beside me. "Sorry to be so late today," she told me, placing a hand lovingly on my cheek. "I needed to find a new route."

She unpacked a bowl of stew and unscrolled a napkin to reveal two jam-filled crêpes. My stomach growled with anticipation.

"A new route?" I asked between bites of crêpe. Mmmm! Red currant preserves—my favorite!

"Mm-hmm." Vivienne pulled a few more things from her magic sack. She held both hands behind her back, asking me to choose one.

I went with right. Vivienne produced a deck of cards.

"Fancy a game of belote?" she asked.

"Yes, please!"

"Ah, but there's still the other hand," she reminded me. She extended her left arm and showed me the other item she was holding.

"A pencil!" I could hardly contain my excitement. It used to be that I couldn't go a day without drawing, but now that I had endured many such days, I knew otherwise. Yet somehow Vivienne had known. Or, more likely, Julien had told her how deeply I loved to draw.

"I couldn't get you any paper just yet, but soon, I hope. I also got you this."

From her skirt pocket she produced a small eraser. I accepted this item as well and spontaneously hugged her.

"Thank you so much! You have no idea how much this means to me."

Vivienne smiled. "I'm glad. I wish I could bring you so much more. Hopefully, soon."

"Soon?" I pounced on the word. "Is there news? Has anything changed?"

She sighed. "No, chérie. But no news is good news, n'est-ce pas? And it is also good news that things have not changed for the worse. So—shall we play?"

"Sure," I said, thankful for the distraction. She dealt, and we played in near silence for a while. I held my cards with one hand and spooned stew into my mouth with the other. If Maman could have seen me now, she'd most certainly have had something to say about this. In normal times, at home, Maman would never have let me play games at the table or eat meals while playing cards.

"No slouching, Sara," she would often say, looking at me pointedly over her glasses.

"And no slurping," Papa would add.

"Yes, that's right," Maman would agree.

But these were not normal times, and however homey the Beaumiers had made the hayloft, it was not a home. Vivienne seemed to sense these things and found ways to make my days more bearable. It wasn't just the food and the small gifts she brought me. It was her. She was a ray of sunshine.

"Ah! You win, chérie!" she cried. "I demand a rematch."

"I suppose . . . if you insist," I joked. We both knew I wouldn't have had it any other way.

It was my turn to deal, and as I did, I realized that Vivienne had not exactly answered my question. "Isn't your house across the road, on the other side of the big field?" I asked, picturing it from the night I first arrived.

"It is."

"Then . . . what did you mean, 'a new route'? Isn't there just one way to get here?"

"Not exactly," said Vivienne, picking up her hand of cards and studying it. "With the Lafleurs next door and their eyes always on the street, I needed to get a little, shall we say, creative."

"Ohhh. . . ." This hadn't occurred to me, but it made sense. If she walked out the front door with her bags filled and made a beeline for the barn but returned with empty sacks, she'd certainly arouse suspicion.

"My route, until today, has been to go to town, as I always have done, and do my shopping. I try to do it as quickly as possible, to leave plenty of time for our visits. Then, when no one is looking, I take a side street that leads away from town in the direction of the Mernuit."

"The forest!" I couldn't help letting my alarm show. She couldn't be serious—could she?

"It's fine, really," Vivienne assured me, taking her turn. "There's a little winding path, through a section that's not particularly dense. And it leads to the grove of trees on the back side of the barn. From there, I can enter the barn without being seen. There's a hole in the wall that I always used to remind Jean-Paul to patch. But he never got around to it, and now I'm glad he didn't!" She laughed, and I smiled, too. Her warmth was infectious.

"But—how did you change your route today? And why?" I asked. I was distracted by the image of her in the forest, walking through thick fog. I didn't like the idea of her putting herself in the path of a wolf for any reason. Vivienne had to point to my hand of cards to remind me that it was my turn.

"When I went down the little street I always take," she answered, "I was watching over my shoulder to make sure no one noticed me. I practically crashed into someone, and when I looked up, I realized it was a German soldier. The Nazis had set up a new checkpoint, right there."

"Vivienne! That's so scary," I said with a shudder.

"It was fine. I just pretended I was lost and retraced my steps. Then I took the next street over and backtracked to get to the forest a kilometer or so later."

"A kilometer? How far out of your way is this route taking you?"

"Not far at all," insisted Vivienne. "Just three kilometers or so. It's fine, really. I like to walk. It's good exercise."

I envied her her freedom. How I wished I could take a walk anywhere. Walk to the Beaumiers' house. Walk to my own house, for that matter. Better yet, fly there like a bird!

"Ah!" said Vivienne as I played my cards. "You win again, chérie!"

I looked down with surprise. I might as well be a bird, since my head was off in the clouds so often these days. These visits from Vivienne helped, though, to ground me.

"I demand another rematch. Tomorrow, shall we say?"

"I'm very busy tomorrow," I replied. "But perhaps I can squeeze you in."

Her eyes sparkled at my joke. Then she gathered her things, kissed me, and climbed down from the hayloft.

"Can you hand me my sacks?" she called up to me.

I obliged, bringing them over to the edge. One sack, as usual, was still heavy with the grocery items Vivienne was going to take home for herself, Jean-Paul, and Julien. As I passed it down, I must have let go too soon.

Crash!

I looked down to see the bag on the ground, its contents spilled. The items included two milk bottles—one of which had shattered in the fall.

"I'm so sorry!" I cried out. "Are you okay?"

"It's fine. I'm fine," Vivienne replied. She picked up the intact milk bottle and wiped it off on her skirt. "No harm done. I'll just pass by the dairy on the way home, don't you worry." She went over to the corner and returned with the broom.

"The . . . dairy?" I looked down at her, confused. Occasionally, I could hear the sound of a cow lowing in the distance. But if there was a dairy close by, I think that I would have known. The sounds—and smells—of a dairy are pretty distinctive.

Vivienne nodded. As she stooped and began picking up the larger pieces of glass carefully, she explained. "To keep the Lafleurs' curious eyes from spotting me, I go home the same way that I get here. Through the back of the barn, then the path through the forest, and back by side roads to the market square." She stood up and got to work with the broom. "If the dairy is open, I'll pick up more milk. That way, I'll have enough for us and the Lafleurs. If the dairy is closed, the Lafleurs can have our milk today. We'll make do."

I stared at Vivienne with admiration as she swept up the last of the debris and packed it into her bag to take with her. I still couldn't believe she was so kind that she would keep bringing them milk, day after day. Shame on the Lafleurs! How could anyone be so heartless as to spy on their neighbors and treat someone as good as Vivienne this way?

She gave a little wave in my direction.

"Until tomorrow, ma petite!"

I waved and watched her leave. She walked over to the back wall and crouched by a hole in the boards, near one corner. Then she slipped through the gap and disappeared from view.

It was only after she was gone that I realized something else.

Her daily "exercise walk" to visit me wasn't three kilometers. She took the same route both ways, bringing the total to six kilometers. And she did this every day, no matter the weather. All to keep her nosy neighbors from getting too curious. All to keep me safe.

After Vivienne left, I organized my day. I decided to tidy up my space and do my exercises. As a reward, I planned to allow myself to read and draw with my new pencil. My "chores" ended up going quickly, as there was little that needed tidying. I stretched and did deep knee bends and tried to remember as many physical fitness challenges as I could from my gym classes. I skipped an imaginary rope to a count of one hundred, did jumping jacks, and walked around my table until I got dizzy. Out of boredom, I decided to teach myself to do handstands against the corner. I had seen boys do this in the schoolyard, but I had never tried myself. When I was finally able to kick my feet all the way up, my skirt fell over my head. But no one could see me, except maybe the bats, so it didn't matter!

Mastering this trick made me feel brave, even as the blood rushed to my head.

"Hey, bats! Look at me!" I called out softly. I kept my voice quiet, though, just in case the wind tried to carry it. I stayed there on my hands for a good ten seconds, grinning the whole time.

Next, I got out my drawing things. Neither the pencil nor the eraser was new—the pencil was decently sharp but stubby, and the eraser was a dark dingy gray. But I was still so pleased to have them. Except . . . without paper, I wasn't sure what to do with them. So, after admiring them some more, I decided to read for a while instead.

My selection of books was somewhat limited. When Vivienne brought reading material for my collection, she often apologized. There was no need—I was glad to have anything to look at, even Julien's dreadful old math book. That's right, my least favorite subject. But thinking of math gave me an idea. I pulled the detested book off the potato-crate shelf and flipped to the back. Sure enough, there were lots of blank pages, provided for working out problems. I was tempted to rip them out but decided instead to just turn the math book into a sketchbook.

I sat down and slowly began to brush the pencil across the page. Soon there was a wing, then another, and before long, I had brought a bird to flight. Then another and another. I added curling vines, flowers, all the beautiful things that lived in my imagination. I put down my pencil and stared at the pages. It was good to have a world I could go to whenever I needed it, a world where everything was peaceful and where flowers could grow and birds fly free. I added another rose and a butterfly. I finally forced myself to stop so I could have some pencil left for another day. The point was now pretty dull, but I knew that Julien could probably sharpen it with his pocketknife.

For the rest of the day, I stared out through the small space between the window boards on the back wall, trying to see actual birds. Some days, I would look out of that tiny sliver of the window for hours on end. Through the glass, I could see the edge of the woods, the fields, and the sky. It reminded me of how lovely the world still was—the real, actual world, not just the world I could create on paper. Even if physically I couldn't go out into it anymore, it was good to know it was there. The Nazis had taken a lot from me, but the sky, and the birds— those were things they couldn't steal. The other thing that they couldn't destroy was my imagination. They could drive me into hiding, but my imagination could still roam free.

I was thankful for that. It was all I had left.

*   *   *

"What about Julien? Did he ever visit you?"

"Bien sûr!" Grandmère told him. "Of course! Every evening. As soon as it started getting dark, my heart would soar because I knew that soon he would be paying me a visit. I looked forward to those visits so much."

"Did he go through town, like his mom?"

She shook her head. "No, Julien would rely on the darkness. Remember, the Lafleurs were elderly and relatively infirm. As soon as it got dark out, they would leave their window and go inside."

"Some spies," scoffed Julian. "You'd think they might have gotten night vision goggles. Or weren't those invented yet?"

"Actually, I think I read somewhere that the Germans developed them during the 1930s. But they weren't widely available. And yes, it was a good thing that the Lafleurs did not have a pair. Because every night, Julien would sneak out his back door, slide around the back of the house his family shared with the Lafleurs, and cross the field to see me."

CHAPTER TWO

"Allô? Sara?"

"Julien!" I scrambled over to the hayloft's edge to greet him. He grinned up at me. "Hi!"

"Hi yourself. Give me a hand?"

"Of course."

"Here, take these." Julien handed his crutches up to me, one at a time. Then he tossed something else up to me.

"Whoa!" I caught the heavy package, which turned out to be his schoolbooks, wrapped in an old shirt. I set them aside and reached down for his wrists to help haul him up.

"Actually, watch this. I think I can . . ." Julien climbed as far as he could on the stacked-up bales of hay that didn't fit in the loft. Then he reached for the edge of the hayloft and determinedly tried to pull himself higher.

"Why don't I brace you, or—"

"It's okay." Julien interrupted me, although not in a rude way. "I want to do this myself."

"Sure." I scooted back to give him room and watched as his

face slowly rose over the edge. It was red from exertion, and I feared what would happen if his arms suddenly gave out. I was just about to lunge forward and grab him when suddenly his right elbow and forearm swung into view. And then his left. With a grunt, he pulled his torso higher until he was able to twist himself into a sitting position on the lip of the hayloft. "Heyyy! You did it!" I cried, bursting into applause.

Julien used his hands to help swing his legs up. I passed him his crutches.

"You didn't think I could do it," he teased.

"I did so! I never doubted you."

He raised one eyebrow accusingly.

"Okay, maybe for a moment I did. But just because you looked like a beet, you were so red in the face." I held my breath and tried to do an impersonation of him struggling at the edge. Then I let out all the air in a hurry, worried I had gone too far and insulted him.

But Julien laughed. "This from the girl who couldn't keep up with a boy on crutches!"

"What, in the sewers?" He was right, of course. But I was enjoying joking around with him. "That was hardly a fair race."

"You're right," he said. "I'll tell you what. Next time, we'll swim."

"You're on," I agreed with a laugh. "I'll beat you fair and square."

"I look forward to that," he said.

"So do I," I retorted. And I almost meant it. I would do almost anything, perhaps even swim in the sewers, to have my freedom back. But the next best thing was having a real friend I could laugh and have a little fun with, and who could take my mind away from this place. For a few hours each night, I could forget about the Nazis, the barn, the bats . . . and just be a kid.

"Speaking of swimming, you should have seen what happened to Pastor Luc today. He was on duty when the little ones had their outdoor playtime, and this boy—I think his name is Pierre?—said he had to use the bathroom. Pastor Luc told him to go ahead, meaning to go inside . . ."

"Oh no," I said, starting to laugh as I guessed where this was going.

"Yup, he went, all right. He went all over Pastor Luc!"

"Oh that's terrible," I said, picturing the scene. I was jealous that Julien still got to go to school every day, and not just because of the funny stories and gossip he brought home for me. I missed everything about school—even math!—and I hated feeling left out and left behind. Julien seemed to know this, so he often brought his assignments. We set up a little classroom in the loft and reviewed whatever had been covered that day.

"Today's math was actually pretty easy. You should have no trouble picking it up," he said.

"Hey, what's that supposed to mean?" I asked.

"Nothing! Though it will be easier if you save a few pages in your book for math." He had pulled his old math book off my shelf, looking for scratch paper presumably, and discovered my sketchbook.

"Julien!"

"I'm just kidding! You know I love your art."

"Thanks." I suddenly felt shy. "They're just little doodles," I added.

"Hardly," he insisted. "Mademoiselle Petitjean said you had a real gift, and she was right."

An awkward silence set in as her name hung in the air.

Finally I broke it. "You haven't heard anything, have you?"

He shook his head. "No one has. They assigned a new teacher to our room, and she just picked up like nothing happened. As if Mademoiselle Petitjean never existed."

I looked down, a lump forming in my throat. Like his mother, Julien seemed to see his job as keeping my spirits up, so he quickly changed the subject.

"Hey, any chance you want to go exploring?"

"Exploring?" I looked at Julien with confusion.

"Not outside," he quickly added. "But I mean, as long as we don't leave the barn, it's probably okay, right?"

I remembered what Vivienne had said the night I arrived. *Once you're up there, please don't come down from the loft for any reason.* And yet, once Julien suggested that I could put my feet on solid ground, I found myself unable to refuse the opportunity.

"Just for a few minutes," I told him.

"Of course. And if we hear anyone coming, there are some places we can hide. I'll show you."

He led the way to the hayloft's edge and lowered himself down. I handed Julien his crutches and followed him.

"Ohhh," I said when my feet finally touched the barn floor. "It feels so good, I want to bend down and kiss the ground!"

"Yeah, I wouldn't do that if I were you," he said. "Maybe let's just wave at it instead?"

So we both bent forward and waved at the floor as if greeting an old friend. "Hi, floor!" I called out. "Oh, how I've missed you."

"You look great, floor," he added jokingly. "It's amazing how strong you are, considering how many people step on you."

I didn't say it, but it crossed my mind that the same could be said for Julien. All those years I had watched so many people ridicule and hurt him, and yet his inner resilience had remained intact.

"Allow me to give you the grand tour," he offered, extending an arm dramatically. I curtsied in acquiescence and followed him as he paraded around, pointing out all the sights. "This is the haystack, and adjacent to it is the supplementary haystack. If you're looking for a needle, you might want to start here. This is a barrel. If it looks familiar, it might be because it is related to a barrel that lives up in the hayloft."

"You're saying this barrel is the uncle of the upstairs barrel?" I suggested.

"I am! The long-lost uncle. He went on a trip to Africa years ago, and he only returned recently. But he hasn't reconnected with his family yet because of his dark secret." His voice shifted to a conspiratorial whisper. "He's filled with rum!"

I made a shocked face. "How did he get to Africa in the first place?" I asked.

"He drove," replied Julien. Then he burst out laughing.

"You're probably wondering how he got to Africa and back by car, and that is indeed an interesting story."

"Some barrels float," I pointed out.

"Yes, they do! And that is exactly what happened. He and his car floated across the Strait of Gibraltar. It was in all the newspapers." He pointed to the rusted-out red car I had noticed when I arrived, the one that was missing some of its tires. "And in fact, this is his historic car!"

"It certainly does look seaworthy," I said.

"Perhaps tomorrow night we could take it for a . . . float?" he proposed.

I grinned. "I would like that very much, Monsieur Beaumier."

And the next night we did just that. The sun set, and a little while later Julien appeared, though without his books this time. I climbed down from the hayloft, and he gallantly opened the car door for me. Then he went around the other side and climbed in.

"Where to tonight, Mademoiselle Blum?" he asked, holding a steering wheel that looked ready to fall off in his hands.

"Hmm . . . ," I said, considering. "This car floats, does it not?"

"Indeed it does. It can take you anywhere you'd like to go. We don't need to limit ourselves to mere roads."

Well, that was music to my ears. Sure, we were sitting in a completely rusted, decrepit old jalopy. But Julien's imagination was as quick as his math skills. So why limit ourselves, indeed?

"Is it true that you like animals, mademoiselle?" he asked.

"I do. Birds, especially."

"Well, I have it on good authority that the animals in Australia are quite exceptional."

"Hmm. That's correct. But I also hoped to go to Africa."

Julien checked an imaginary watch. "If we hurry, we can make it to both! But we might want to take a different vehicle for that."

I looked at him. "Like . . . a submarine?"

"I was thinking a magic flying car."

"How about a magic flying chariot made of gold?"

"Done!" he announced, pretending to rev the engine. "Full speed ahead!"

Since there was no glass in the windows, it was easy to stick my head out as he "drove." I could practically feel the wind in my hair as we flew through the sky. We took turns pointing out sights to each other . . . my house, Notre-Dame Cathedral, the Taj Mahal—what can I say? It was an unusual route—and out of the blue we spotted our first kangaroos. From there, it was off to Africa, where a safari awaited us.

"Careful, Julien! Don't drive into that rhino over there!" I cried out, grabbing his arm.

"I see it! But I have to avoid the quicksand to the right."

We leaned back and forth, dodging hurdles and dreaming up new ones. Our adventure ended far too soon when Jean-Paul appeared in the doorway to remind Julien that he had school the next day. If he found it alarming that I was downstairs, or odd that we were playing in the old car, he didn't let on. And for that I was grateful.

"I'll be along in a minute, Papa," Julien told him.

Jean-Paul nodded and left.

Julien waited as I carefully climbed back up to my hayloft. Usually, we just silently waved good night, but this evening I called out his name as he started to leave.

"Yes?"

"I— Thank you."

"Thank you," he replied. "If you hadn't spotted that rhino, I would be a dead man."

"Oh, go on, you saw it, too," I said. "But really, that was so much fun."

"It was fun for me as well," he said. "It probably sounds silly to you, but I never really get to play with anyone like that."

"Neither do I," I admitted.

"Yes, you do," he said. "You have lots of friends at school."

I smiled wistfully, thinking of Mariann and Sophie. But I told him the truth. "I don't have anyone who will play with me that way. My friends back home wouldn't be anywhere near as good at it. Or they'd think I was babyish for wanting to make up games like that."

"I guess. But still, it must be nice to have friends. I wish I did."

"You do," I told him. "You have me."

Julien grinned. Then he gave a little wave and ducked out the door.

* * *

I went over to the window and stared out at the moon. I tried to make the barn walls fade away so I could feel that feeling of riding in a magic chariot with Julien again. Roaming through the skies all around the world, wild and free.

After a while, I got into my bed. I wrapped my blanket tightly around me, closed my eyes, and inhaled its comforting lavender scent. Some nights, this would work and I would fall asleep right away.

But that night? I was not so lucky. It was dark in the hayloft, but moonlight found a way to creep in. The shadows danced spookily, and every so often a bat would dart out to chase a moth or some other tasty flying treat. My eyes flew open when I heard their shrill, squeaky cries. I looked around anxiously, but I couldn't quite make them out since they were so high above my head. I waited in vain for my nocturnal roommates to settle down, but their shadowy shapes were constantly shifting, like a big amorphous dark cloud.

And dark clouds made me think of mist. I pictured the dense fog of the forest, where the wolves were said to hide, crouched to attack. I saw their red eyes, glowing like jewels and piercing through the thick fogbanks. I tried with all my might to push those thoughts away. Wolves couldn't climb up to my hayloft, I reminded myself. I was safe from them. Again I closed my eyes and tried to drift off. . . .

Arooooooooo!

This time, I bolted upright. I felt the hot breath of the animal in my face, and I recoiled in terror that somehow it had tracked me down.

I blinked, and looked around.

No wolf.

But I had heard a wolf, all right, and I shouldn't have been surprised—the Mernuit forest was right next to the barn. Otherwise, Vivienne would not have been able to take her secret path to visit me each day. But was the howl I heard coming from an actual wolf, prowling in the woods outside the barn? Or was it a wolf in my dreams, haunting me and daring me to return to sleep so it could finish me off?

Both wolves seemed very real to me. And I wasn't willing to take my chances with either one.

I lay awake for hours, staring up at the bats and waiting for morning to come.

"How long did you have to stay in the barn?" asked Julian.

"Well, in the beginning, I couldn't believe I would survive up there for even a few weeks," Grandmère told him. "Before long, though, I settled into a routine and accepted the fact that this was my life now— for however long I had to live that way."

Julian shook his head in apparent disbelief. "Did you ever get mad at Julien?" he asked. "Or, like, get jealous that he could come and go whenever he wanted, but you were just stuck there?"

Grandmère considered Julian's question for a moment. "I missed my life before, of course. But by the summertime, the barn had become my whole world. And Julien was the center of that world."

"Like a best friend?"

She nodded eagerly. "Yes, but also more. He was my companion, my confidant, my co-conspirator. The two of us were like, you know, two peas in a pod."

A funny look crossed Julian's face.

"Did I say it wrong?" Grandmère asked with concern. Despite being bilingual, she sometimes got tripped up by English expressions. " 'Peas in a pod,' no? By which I mean that we were the same."

"You said it right," Julian assured her. "Sorry, it's just—from the way you described him, I figured he was pretty different from you."

"He looked different from me," his grandmother replied. "But inside? We were the same."

CHAPTER THREE
Summer 1943

On the weekends, Julien would sometimes take Vivienne's route through town and pay me a visit during the day. One steamy Saturday in August, Julien had come to see me and the two of us were passing the afternoon together in our usual manner. We had reached a comfortable new stage in our friendship, where we didn't always need to be talking. It made me realize that the best friendships are the ones in which words are not needed. I was deeply engrossed in the book I was reading when a soft rhythmic sound caught my attention. I followed the sound to Julien, who was sitting on the opposite end of my hay mattress. He appeared to be sharpening a pencil or peeling an apple—I couldn't tell which.

"What are you working on?" I asked.

"A slingshot," he replied.

"A slingshot?" I repeated with alarm. "What on earth would you use that for?"

"Big game," he replied, not looking up from his work. "For our next safari. One never knows when a rhino might charge."

"I thought we were going to visit a new planet next time," I said, a smile dancing on my lips.

"Good point. But those outer-space rhinos can be particularly fierce."

"I've heard that, too," I said.

"How's the math homework going?" Julien asked.

"Perfect. Fantastic. I finished it hours ago," I lied, in the most obvious way.

"Oh, really? That's wonderful. Can I see?" he asked, calling my bluff.

I flopped flat on the floor dramatically. "Ugh. This is just not fair. I don't know why you're making me do math in the summer. I'm terrible at it!" I gave him my best pout for full effect.

"I'm not making you do it," he pointed out patiently. "I'm encouraging you to do it, so you can keep up. For when—"

"You mean if!" I interrupted, daring him to bicker with me.

"When," he repeated calmly, refusing to take the bait. "When you come back to school. Come on—math isn't so bad. If you keep working at it, you'll get it."

"Easy for you to say. You're a math genius!"

Julien scoffed. "I'm not a genius! I just paid attention in class. You were always too busy doodling all those birds to pay attention."

"Wait! You saw my bird drawings?"

"Of course, silly! I sat next to you for three years! How could I not notice what you were doodling?"

I suddenly felt shy. My parents, friends, and teachers had

often complimented my art, and their admiration added to the joy and pride I felt when I drew pictures. But a lot of my confidence and happiness had evaporated when Vincent looked at my sketchbook. It made me nauseous to remember his bitter words and how much they had upset me. I knew he was wrong, but his insult was like a seed that took root, sprouting little tendrils of self-doubt. Maybe I wasn't a good artist? Maybe I wasn't a good anything? I knew the Nazis weren't right about me—they didn't even know me! But deep inside I worried: What if they were?

"Why did you always draw birds, anyway?" asked Julien, his innocent question bringing me back.

"I don't know," I admitted. "I just like birds, I guess." But something about the look on his face, genuinely curious and interested in me, made me say more. "I suppose it also has to do with . . . a game Papa and I used to play when I was little. It's silly, really."

"Silly? Oh, now you have to tell me."

"You're going to laugh. It was very childish," I told him.

"I won't laugh," he promised.

"Well . . ." I hesitated, but when I looked into his eyes, it felt like I was looking through him, and through the hayloft, to another place. A place I knew very well: the fairy flower field of the Mernuit. And so I began to tell him about our game.

"When I was a little girl, I would go for picnics with my parents in the forest every spring. There's this spot my papa found, this little grove that's just completely overgrown with bluebells. Have you ever seen that?"

Julien shook his head.

"Oh, I really hope you do someday. It's the most magical thing! To me, it always felt like the forest floor had transformed into a sea of blooming purple overnight. I'd run around, pretending I was a fairy in an enchanted garden, and sing and dance. It was my favorite place."

For a moment I was swept up in the memory. I could almost feel the gentle spring breezes and the intoxicating floral scent of the bluebells. I saw Maman, setting out our lunch on the picnic blanket. And Papa, looking elegant and smart and gazing at me adoringly.

"Every time we went there," I told Julien, "we would play this game. We made it up, but it was so long ago that I don't even remember when. We'd pretend that I was a little bird getting ready to fly."

I spread my arms wide, imagining my papa hoisting me above his head.

"My papa would lift me up high. And he'd spin me around and say, 'How high will you fly?'"

I heard his voice, echoing in my head as I joined him, reciting both parts for Julien.

"And I'd answer, 'As high as the sky!'"

I twirled in place, lost in the memory.

"And my papa would ask, 'How fast will you go?' and I'd tell him, 'As fast as a crow!'

"And then he'd tell me, 'Close your eyes. . . . Time to rise!'"

I closed my eyes and spun some more, not wanting to come down from the sky . . . or back from the memory. Finally, I opened my eyes. The hayloft swam into view, and there was Julien. He was staring at me, a bemused grin on his face.

"I told you it was silly," I said, suddenly embarrassed. I had never told anyone about that.

"Aww! Not at all. That's completely charming!"

I snuck a look at him to see if he was laughing at me. But he seemed sincere. "Yeah, I guess," I said.

"Perhaps your papa can make me fly someday, too," suggested Julien.

I smiled wistfully at that thought. Who knew if my papa would make anyone fly again? Even me.

"Yeah, maybe," I said, feeling my sadness return. "If I ever see him again."

"Don't say that, Sara. You'll see him again. I know it."

He was serious, which was reassuring to me. And for a moment, he had me convinced. Except I knew Julien was just a kid, like me. And even the adults, what did they know? Every day, I asked Vivienne for news about my family, but so far she had not produced even one crumb of information. It was as if they had disappeared, poof!, with the wave of a magician's wand. But not a good magician; an evil one who had no intention of pulling them out of his hat with a flourish.

So I asked, "How can you know?"

Julien was unwavering. "I just do, that's all. There are some things we know in our hearts. This is one of them. You will see your father again, Sara. I know it."

I sighed and sat down again. "I sure hope you're right, Julien."

Julien went over to my books and selected a volume. "And because I know that day is coming, I know he'll be very cross with me if I let you fall behind on your math." He handed me the math book and took a seat near me. "So back to work, young lady!"

"Ugh!" I groaned in weak protest. But inside I felt grateful. Grateful for normal things—even math, which I detested—to take my mind off my bigger worries. And grateful to have a friend who always found a way to make me feel better, no matter what. A friend who gave me hope when otherwise there would be none. A friend who brought light into my darkest of days.

I kept wanting to tell him how much I appreciated him. It wasn't just that he'd saved my life. He'd saved my very being. But every time I tried to rehearse what to say to him, the words seemed awkward and inadequate. Ultimately, I had to admit defeat. How could mere words possibly convey what Julien was starting to mean to me?

CHAPTER FOUR
Fall 1943

"Sara!"

I sat up in surprise, ran to the hayloft's edge, and peered down. "Julien? You're here so early today! Is everything okay?" It was extra exciting to me because it was the fall, so Julien had just started back to school. I was eager to hear everything about his classes and my friends, but I had assumed I would need to wait until nightfall.

He nodded, and I noticed that although he was balanced as usual on his crutches, both of his hands were behind his back. "I have a surprise," he said. "Come down, and close your eyes. That is, come down with your eyes open. Then close your eyes!"

"All right," I said, lowering myself down to the haystack and onto the barn floor. I stood in front of him, grinning eagerly. I loved surprises! When Papa used to travel to give medical lectures, he would sometimes bring home what he called "little treasures" for me. Hair ribbons, and once a box of perfect pink macarons from Ladurée, a famous Parisian tea room.

"Close your eyes and hold out your hands," said Julien, trying to sound stern. "And no peeking!" he added.

"I'm not peeking!" I told him. And I wasn't, really!

I felt him place something flat in my hands. A book? I was tempted to sneak a look, but before I could, Julien said, "Okay, now you can open your eyes."

I looked down at what I was holding.

And gasped.

"My sketchbook? Oh, Julien—" I was speechless. Talk about a treasure! I turned it over in my hands, marveling that it was indeed my book, which I had left behind along with my coat and boots and everything else on that awful day. I flipped it open and was rewarded with a flurry of my birds. They seemed as delighted to see me as I was to see them. "But—but how?" I finally asked.

He shrugged like it was no big deal, even though I could tell he was pleased with my response. "I was in Pastor Luc's office today, and—"

"Oh no! What were you doing in Pastor Luc's office?" I asked with concern. Pastor Luc rarely called students into his office. When he did, it was usually because they had misbehaved. That didn't sound like Julien, but I worried nonetheless.

"Nothing bad," he assured me. "He just wanted to tell me that they're moving me up to advanced mathematics this year."

"Julien, that's wonderful! Congratulations!"

"Thanks! That's what Pastor Luc said." He pulled himself up to his full height on his crutches and adjusted an imaginary pair of spectacles. "Congratulations, young man. You'll be with the older students. They've already been told and know to welcome you."

"Thank you, Pastor Luc," I told him, tipping a pretend cap in return. If Julien could play Pastor Luc, I could certainly play Julien.

He grinned at my impression and continued to tell the story in his own voice. "So as I turned to leave, I noticed something familiar on Pastor Luc's desk. I almost asked if I could have it—you know, I figured I could say it was something to remember you by?—but I immediately worried that would attract unwanted attention."

"You don't think Pastor Luc is . . . ?"

Julien shook his head. "No, he's not a Nazi. But you know our school. People talk. Word could get around, and we wouldn't want that."

"That was smart of you," I told him. "So how did you get it?"

"Well, as you know, I often leave after everyone else. If people see me, they just assume it must be because I use crutches. They have no idea how speedy I am when I want to be."

I smiled. "I'll admit it. Before I got to know you, I had no idea you were a race car driver."

Julien looked pleased. "Yes, well, this time it was an advantage to have people think I'm a slowpoke. I waited until everyone had gone home for the day; then I snuck into Pastor Luc's office. I tucked your sketchbook into my shirt and carried it all the way home."

"My hero!" I said, and I meant it.

"I'm glad it makes you happy. I knew it would! I was so excited to bring it to you, I came straight here."

I glanced out one of the boarded-up windows nervously. "But . . . Julien, it's not quite dark out yet. What if someone saw you?"

"I was careful," he assured me. "I took the forest path, like my maman always does. And when I got to the barn, I peeked around the front just to make sure. But the Lafleurs, for once, were not at their window."

"That was very brave of you."

"I can be very brave when the situation calls for it," he said proudly.

"Thank you," I said. And I couldn't help what happened next. I reached out and wrapped my arms around his neck in an appreciative hug. He seemed startled at first, but he hugged me back. I rested my head on his surprisingly strong shoulders and breathed in deeply. Hay, soap, and a touch of sweat, but not in a bad way. I wished I could tell my school friends how good he actually smelled. And how wonderful holding him felt.

Time seemed to stand still for a moment. But I worried that I was being too forward, so I pulled back. Julien did as well.

"Um . . . ," he said awkwardly.

I looked down, suddenly feeling shy. My stomach was doing flips for some reason. "Umm . . . yeah, so thanks," I said.

"Sure."

Was it strange that I hugged him? Did I make him uncomfortable? I wondered. Think of something to say! I told myself.

Something normal, to set him at ease again. "Uh . . . so I was—" I stammered clumsily.

"Wait. Did you hear that?"

Unfortunately, I did.

"Shh!" Julien leaned in and cupped his hand around my ear. "Go back up to the loft and hide," he whispered. "Don't come out, no matter what. Hurry!"

I scrambled up to the loft, wishing Julien had waited just a little bit longer before coming to see me. The darkness was closing in, but not fast enough. I jumped into my bed, covering my head with the blanket. A moment later, I sat up again. A person-sized lump in the bed? Too obvious! I looked around frantically, but my options were limited. The table had no cloth. There were barrels, but they were closed on both ends, so hiding inside one wouldn't work. Finally, I spotted the only place that offered a chance of invisibility: the hay pile at the far end of the loft, beneath the rafters. This was the area I always avoided because of the bats. But I knew it was the most well-hidden. I dug myself a hole and quickly pulled the hay around me, obscuring my face and body. Then I wriggled until I got close to the edge of the hayloft. This way, I could remain hidden but have a decent view of the barn floor below. I wanted to wave to Julien to show him where I was and assure him that I was okay. But if I moved, I might knock the hay out of the way and ruin my hiding place.

I stayed as still as I could and watched Julien from my perch. He glanced up in my direction, almost as if he knew I could see him. Then he went over to the car. Our magic flying golden chariot. I watched as he opened the hood and looked inside. It seemed like he was trying to fix the engine, which made no sense. The car didn't even have four tires, and the ones it had were flat.

But when I heard the voices again, I realized why he needed to pretend he was in the barn for a reason, like fixing the engine. The voices were getting louder.

Whoever was outside the barn was coming inside.

CHAPTER FIVE

The voices were coming closer. My heart beat faster and faster, as I was certain it was the notorious Lafleurs. Surely they had seen Julien and alerted their fellow Nazis. The nearer they got to the barn, the more I could make out their words.

"Boy, that cripple can move fast. Where'd he go?"

"Into the barn, I think."

To my horror, I recognized one of the voices. It was Vincent. I wanted to call down to Julien, to warn him and tell him to sneak out the hole in the back corner of the barn. But I couldn't, not without risking being heard and bringing Vincent and his creepy friends into the barn to investigate.

"Maybe he went into his house?" said another voice. It was probably Jérôme or Paul. Vincent was rarely without his henchmen, who always seemed eager to stir up trouble.

"I'm telling you, he went into this barn."

"Both of you, shut up," snapped Vincent. "You're talking too loud."

"It looks abandoned," one of the other boys replied.

There was a silence. I saw the beam of their flashlight through the slits in the boarded-up windows, presumably as they regarded the barn and tried to decide whether to bother searching it. *Walk away, walk away, walk away,* I silently willed them.

To my immense relief, it seemed to work. One of the boys said, in a voice that sounded surprisingly nervous, "Maybe we should just forget this, Vincent."

"We're not forgetting this," Vincent insisted. "I saw that little cripple take something from Pastor Luc's office . . . and he's going to pay for it, trust me."

Creeeeak . . .

The barn door slowly opened and three dark shapes lumbered inside. Their flashlight beam danced around the room, from the rafters back down to the floor. I tried not to move, praying that Julien had silently slipped out the back.

"Oh, hi, Vincent. Jérôme. Paul." No such luck, I realized when I heard Julien greet them. I looked down and saw him still standing in front of the car's open hood. Julien was highlighted by Vincent's flashlight, and he held his own lantern, which was usually stored with the barn tools. It was clear he was trying his best to sound casual and unconcerned, like their visit was a welcome surprise. "What are you guys doing here?" he asked calmly.

"No, no," said Vincent, shaking his free hand at Julien. "You don't get to ask the questions, you little thief. We saw you take something from Pastor Luc's office. We followed you here." He pointed accusingly at Julien. The other boys grunted and nodded in agreement.

My heart was now like a drum in my ears. I don't know what I would have done if I had been in Julien's shoes. But somehow, he kept his cool. "Yeah, I did—a book I left in his office," he said, sounding nonchalant. "So what?"

"So what?" Vincent echoed Julien's words as if they themselves were a crime. "I don't believe you, that's what."

"I can show it to you," said Julien. Now I truly felt panicked. What if he did show Vincent my sketchbook? In my haste to hide, I hadn't carried it back to the loft with me. Vincent would instantly know it was my art—that Jew's art!—and I'd be discovered, no matter how well I hid. Julien continued breezily, "It's in my house just across the—"

It suddenly dawned on me that of course Julien had no intention of showing them my sketchbook. I was so proud of his quick thinking that I didn't realize what was about to happen. Vincent grabbed Julien roughly by the shoulder. He was a full head taller, with the broad shoulders of a man and a significant weight advantage over poor Julien.

"I told you I don't believe you!" Vincent bellowed.

"Hey, let go of me!" Julien twisted to free himself, but it was no use.

"Give me what you stole or you'll regret it," ordered Vincent.

I could see Jérôme and Paul lurking behind him, adding

their muscle to the equation. Three against one—far from a fair fight, even if the one had been fully able-bodied. A lesser person would have cowered, but Julien stood firm.

"I didn't steal anything," he maintained. "Pastor Luc lent me a book, that's all. I'll lend it to you, too, if you want to read it."

"Are you trying to be funny?" asked Vincent, still holding Julien firmly by the shoulder.

"No."

"I think you are. Get a load of this, guys. Tourteau here is a funny one, isn't he? A veritable riot!"

"Hilarious," said Jérôme flatly.

"Funny-looking," added Paul, making the others dissolve into laughter.

"Be nice, be nice," murmured Vincent, though kindness was obviously the furthest thing from his mind. He studied Julien, like a cat might examine a mouse whose tail it had pinned under one large paw. "You're a really funny kid, aren't you, Tourteau?" he asked. "Joking around like you and Pastor Luc are pals, drinking tea together and swapping books, all cozy like."

"That's not what I said."

Julien's refusal to bow down seemed to set Vincent off again. He passed his flashlight to one of his henchmen, then grabbed Julien's collar with his free hand. He slid his grip from Julien's shoulder to his neck so he was now holding Julien tightly with both hands. I feared he might be choking him, but Julien showed no sign of discomfort. Vincent leaned in, spitting his words into Julien's face. "You think you're smarter than everyone, don't you?" he yelled.

"No, I don't," replied Julien softly.

Vincent scoffed at this response. "They're only putting you into advanced mathematics because they pity you, because you're deformed! You're pathetic and weak! You shouldn't even be allowed to attend a school with decent people, you know that?"

At this point Julien seemed to have concluded that denying these evil lies wasn't worth his breath. He didn't answer but defiantly held Vincent's gaze, face to face. It was unsettling to me that he could. I wondered: In his life, had he experienced worse tormenting even than this?

"You are barely even a person at all. No, you know what you are? A crab. A weak, twisted little crab," announced Vincent. "And you know what the Nazis do with your kind? Inferior little crabs posing as human beings?"

Julien stared back, unafraid.

"They exterminate them. Like the vermin you are. Just like they're doing to the Jews."

His words chilled me to the bone. He had said so many awful and untrue things—how was I to know if this was another of his cruel lies or not? But he wasn't done yet.

"And that's what they'll do to you. That's what I'm going to do to you . . . right now."

It happened fast, like the strike of a cobra. Vincent made a fist, pulled back, and threw a punch that landed squarely on Julien's cheek with a sickening thud. I very nearly cried out in pain on his behalf, but I forced myself to swallow my scream. Julien's body twisted sideways from the force of the blow, so he landed on the ground on his front.

"Get up, you pathetic cripple," said Vincent, kicking Julien with his boot. Julien recoiled, then lay flat again.

Leave! You've done enough harm here! I thought-wished-prayed. But just as I had been unable to use my mental powers to stop them from entering the barn in the first place, I was powerless to end Vincent's assault on Julien. He grabbed Julien from behind by his suspenders and lifted him into an awkward position, dangling like a marionette.

"Lookee here, boys!" Vincent called to the others. "I've hooked myself a crustacean! Not much meat on it, but good eating nonetheless." Jérôme and Paul chuckled appreciatively. "Let's see you crawl like the disgusting crab you are," Vincent said to Julien, pulling him back and forth in an effort to make him dance like a puppet.

"Hey, uh, Vincent?" Jérôme piped up.

Jérôme, thank you! I felt a rush of gratitude. Finally, someone was going to put a stop to this torture!

"Um, yeah . . . heh, heh, maybe we should go now?" This came from Paul, the smaller and twitchier of Vincent's junior thugs. He and Jérôme looked at each other, shifting from foot to foot nervously. Paul's voice sounded squeaky, like he was suddenly realizing the situation might be getting out of hand. Clearly, neither boy had magically grown a conscience. Rather, they both obviously wanted to leave the scene before someone else came along and they had to answer for Vincent's actions.

Vincent responded by putting both hands in the air, as if to show them that he meant no harm. But of course, he had been holding Julien's suspenders, so when he let go, Julien crumpled in a heap on the ground. Vincent turned and leaned over Julien. I thought for a moment that he might spit on Julien as a final offensive gesture. But instead he grabbed Julien's throat and lifted him closer.

"People like you shouldn't be alive," he declared. Then he hauled off and landed another blow on Julien's face. Blood sprayed from Julien's mouth and nose in a bright red arc. Julien let out a moan of pain when the punch landed. The awful wet sounds made me wonder if his nose or jaw were broken. And worst of all, I heard Vincent mutter something under his breath, and all three of those monsters laughed as Julien lay there bleeding at their feet.

At that moment, I knew I could not stay quiet any longer. It felt like I was witnessing the maquisard's murder all over again, and that I could not do. Once was bad enough. I knew only too well how this might unfold if no one stopped Vincent's rampage.

Quickly, I considered my options. I could scream, or throw something like a hay bale off the edge of the loft. That would momentarily distract Vincent and perhaps stop the attack on Julien, but it would likely result in both of us receiving beatings or worse. No, I had to think of something else. I racked my brain frantically. If only Vivienne or Jean-Paul or both of them ever came to the barn at night. They were adults—they could stop this. Had they noticed that Julien had never made it home from school? Were they perhaps out looking for him now? If so, they probably would have started at the barn. And wishing for them to come to the rescue was clearly not going to make them magically appear. *Think, think, think!*

My brain was stuck on Julien's parents. I had to alert them, even if it meant the Germans finding me. I quietly shifted my body, parted the hay, and started getting up.

Just hang on, Julien, I silently told him. *I'm going to go get help.*

There was something about me and Julien at this point, though. A sort of connection beyond words. It often felt like I could read his thoughts, and I later wondered if in this moment he read mine. Because as I peeked over the top of the wall of hay bales, I heard a sound coming from Julien.

"V-*v-v* . . ."

It must have hurt to make any noise, considering what Vincent had done to him. And the blood on Julien's face, coupled with his refusal to keep silent, served as a red cape before this rampaging bull.

"What did you say?" roared Vincent, grabbing Julien's neck once more.

I leaned forward to cry out in protest.

"V-*vive* . . ."

But the voice I heard was not my own. It was Julien's.

"Vive *l'humanité!*"

That triumphant cry took me by surprise. It was louder and more forceful than anything I could have produced, yet it came from deep inside a boy who had been pummeled within an inch of his life.

And that's when it happened.

Floosh! Flap-flap-flap. . . . *Scree! Scree! Scree!*

Suddenly, without warning, hundreds of bats flew out from the rafters and swarmed the barn below. They flew everywhere, shrieking, whooshing through the air like some dark, unholy wind.

"What the—" Vincent looked up, his hands still wrapped around Julien's neck. The air—not just in the hayloft but all through the barn—was thick with bats. Darting, dodging, diving bats, and the shadows of bats in flight, everywhere you looked.

Vincent and his henchmen ran screaming from the barn. I would say they screamed like little girls, but frankly that is an insult to little girls. They screamed like cowards. Evil, cruel cowards.

"Julien! I'm coming down!" I called, as soon as the coast was clear.

I pushed my way through the wall of hay and lowered myself to the barn floor. Quickly, I poked my head outside—under other circumstances, this would have been a rare luxury, but I couldn't allow myself to enjoy it. I looked left and right before closing the door firmly and running to check on Julien.

He was lying on the floor next to the car. Initially I feared the worst. After all, those had been the maquisard's final words. I couldn't let them be Julien's, too.

"Where does it hurt? What can I—"

"Sara, you need to stay in the loft!" replied Julien. He looked at me through eyes that it seemed he could barely open. "They might come back."

Ignoring him, I ran to get his crutches. Then I stood

behind him and tried to help lift him to a position where he could balance on them. "They're gone. I checked. I was about to come out of hiding when the bats—"

"Are you stupid?" Julien snapped. He sounded uncharacteristically angry. "Go up to the loft already!"

Had the beating affected his brain? "I don't care if they catch me!" I told him. "I just want to help."

"But it's not just about you!" yelled Julien in frustration. "Don't you see that? If they find you, they'll arrest my parents. They'll execute them!"

I stared at him, dumbfounded. "Oh, I didn't know. I mean, I didn't realize. . . ."

Now I could see the tears running down Julien's face and mixing with the blood, causing long pink trails to appear. "No, of course you didn't realize!" he blurted out, his voice cracking. "Because you're so self-absorbed! And childish! You're still the same snobby girl who sat next to me for three years and never talked to me! Not even once. . . ."

"Julien, please. I'm sorry," I said. How could I be so stupid? Thinking all the time about how bad I had it, and forgetting that Julien and his family were waiting on me hand and foot. And putting their lives at risk for me, a horrible creature who spent years treating their son like he was a piece of garbage. Or a smelly, scuttling crab. I lowered my head, feeling the weight of my guilt. When it got right down to it, was I any better than Vincent?

"You're still the same girl who never even knew my name. Just go back to the loft, Sara."

I watched Julien turn his crutches and hobble out of the barn.

I stood there, wishing the floor of the barn would swallow me up. And all I could think of was that he was right: I was a monster, just like the Nazis claimed. How else could it be that I had inflicted so much harm on the person who meant the most to me in the world? Despite all I had seen Julien endure, from the bullying at school to this violent and brutal attack, this was the first time I had seen him shed a tear.

I climbed back up to the loft, trying hard not to cry. *You don't deserve to feel sorry for yourself,* I told myself bitterly. Julien was the one who had suffered—not me—and I was the cause of much of his pain.

I lay in my bed that night staring up at the rafters and holes in the roof as I always did. Silently, I thanked the bats for coming out of the woodwork at precisely the right moment. I didn't know what had made them burst forth like they did. We were uneasy roommates at best, so I had no reason to think they were looking out for my interests. But I felt profoundly grateful that in a moment of need, they had done what I was obviously incapable of: helping Julien.

CHAPTER SIX

"I think Pastor Luc should have kicked Vincent out of school,"
I told Vivienne. It was the following day, and we were sitting
together, my head on her shoulder and her comforting arm
around my back. I was still shaken by the events of the previous
night, and she knew it. She patted my hands and spoke softly
into my hair, like Maman did when I was little.

"Between you and me, I agree," she confided. "And in normal times, that's what might have happened. But you know,
maybe it's better this way? Once Pastor Luc tells Vincent's
father that any further problems will be grounds for expulsion,
the threat will keep Vincent in check. And Pastor Luc will be
able to keep a close eye on him."

"He shouldn't just be scolded and watched. He should be
punished!" I insisted. "What about going to the police? Surely
it's still a crime to attack someone for no reason!"

Vivienne looked demoralized. "You're right, Sara, of
course," she replied. "But Jean-Paul and I discussed this last
night, and ultimately we decided it was too risky to report it to

the police. That's why we went to see Pastor Luc this morning instead."

"And after he heard what happened, Pastor Luc didn't think you should go to the police?"

"Actually, he did," admitted Vivienne.

"You see? It's the right thing to do!"

Vivienne shook her head. "I'm sorry, Sara, but we just can't. Vincent's father is connected to the Nazis, so the risk of retaliation is simply too great."

"Oh," I said. I knew there were rumors about Vincent and his family's affiliations, and hearing them confirmed triggered a fresh wave of guilt. Not only had my presence resulted in Julien getting attacked and nearly killed, but I was the reason this crime couldn't even be reported.

"Even though he didn't automatically expel Vincent, Pastor Luc took the situation very seriously," Vivienne added. "He was clearly horrified by what Jean-Paul and I told him. He even went so far as to apologize, as if he were responsible in some way—which is simply not the case. I think that as a man of faith, he finds it difficult to reconcile what is going on around us with his belief in a just and compassionate God."

I nodded silently.

"Pastor Luc seems to believe that before things get worse, God will come to his senses and intervene," continued Vivienne. "I told him, with all due respect, we cannot wait for miracles. Evil will only be stopped when good people decide to put an end to it. It is our fight, not God's."

"You said that?" I asked, surprised. Vivienne was so

cheerful and kind, I didn't realize she was capable of saying something so confrontational. Especially to a man of God.

Vivienne gave me a small smile. "Someone needed to. Although you shouldn't think of me as too much of a radical. Pastor Luc might have been shocked by my candor, but he would never report me to anyone."

"That's good," I said. It was horrible living in a world where so few people could be trusted. And the Beaumier family probably wouldn't have had to worry about such things were it not for me. "I'm sorry," I told Vivienne. "I never realized how much danger I was putting you and Jean-Paul in by being here."

"Oh, chérie, don't worry about us. We'll be fine. Just like you will be, too."

"What about Julien?" I asked. "Will he be fine?" When he'd hobbled out the night before, I'd feared he might not survive. All those blows, and to a body already compromised by his illness.

"Yes, that boy is stronger than all of us, trust me," said Vivienne. "But we need to give him time to heal. Both his body and his heart."

I looked down in shame. Julien must have told his parents everything. Not just about what Vincent had done to him, but what I had done as well. "He got so mad at me," I whispered.

"He was just mad at himself, chérie," Vivienne said, hugging me closer. "For leading Vincent to the barn. The truth is, he should not have taken the sketchbook. It was too risky—for all of us. He knows that. But he couldn't help himself. He saw it and he knew how much it meant to you. But because he was so eager to surprise you, he forgot to be as careful as he should have been. It was a mistake. I don't begrudge him that."

"I know. I just feel like I don't deserve his thoughtfulness. After . . . everything." I knew Julien had probably told her about the way I had ignored him and snubbed him for years. But I couldn't bring myself to say it. And I couldn't believe that even knowing what I had done, she was so willing to show me love and compassion.

She tucked a stray lock of my hair behind my ear and looked into my eyes. "Of course you deserve it," she told me. "In these dark times, it's those small acts of kindness that keep us alive, after all. They remind us of our humanity."

"Vive l'humanité?" I asked.

"Vive l'humanité." Ever since the day I heard the maquisard say those words, I had associated them with conflict, resistance, and defiance. But the way Vivienne said them, they seemed to have another meaning. They were softer—less like a soaring hawk and more like a nesting dove. I tried to hold on to that image as I waited for Julien to be well enough to return to the barn.

And as I hoped that when he was well enough, he would want to return to the barn.

"Sara?"

I sat up, startled by the sound of my name. I had been asleep, but I hoped I wasn't dreaming. The voice I heard saying it was the voice I had been waiting to hear for two weeks.

They had been the longest and loneliest two weeks of my life. I had dutifully tried to think up ways to pass the time. I read. I drew. And I thought. That was the problem, actually. I couldn't stop thinking about the things Julien had said to me.

Two weeks was an awfully long time to be alone with those thoughts. Especially since I knew that Julien was right—all this time, in the barn, I had been thinking only about myself. Even though I no longer cared about having pretty red shoes or playing my piano pieces or having Papa bring me treasures from his travels, I was still the spoiled little girl I had always been. But the hardest part about Julien's extended absence wasn't coming to terms with my own embarrassment and remorse about my behavior. The hardest part was realizing that I might never see Julien again and might never have the chance to tell him just how sorry I was.

"Julien?" I called out, rushing to the hayloft's edge. "Hi. Should I come down?"

"No, I'll come up."

"Okay."

He handed up his crutches, and I waited as he carefully hauled himself up to the loft. I almost offered to help, but he looked more determined than ever. And I sort of worried that if I said anything, I'd break the spell and he'd leave again. He looked tired and his face still had some cuts and bruises, but otherwise he seemed like himself. That was a big relief.

"What have you been up to?" he asked.

"Not much," I said truthfully. "How about you?"

"School. Homework. You know."

I waited, hoping for more details. But I got none. It crossed my mind that perhaps he didn't even want to come see me. Maybe Vivienne had put him up to it.

I opened my mouth to ask. But then I shut it again. I didn't want to know the answer. And I was grateful to have him visit, even if it was out of obligation rather than by choice.

"Do you want to . . . go for a drive?" I asked.

Julien shook his head.

"Or . . . we could do some math?" I suggested. "I know I need to stay on top of it, so—"

"Maybe another time," he said.

I glanced around quickly, afraid he'd be gone before too much longer if I didn't come up with some way of engaging his interest.

"What about cards?"

Julien shrugged indifferently. "Okay," he said.

"Fantastic. I'll deal!" I plopped down on the floor and began shuffling. I didn't even have to ask, because our default game was Julien's favorite: belote.

He won the first round. And the second. And the third.

"Another round?" he asked.

"Okay." In all honesty, I'd had enough of playing cards. But since it was all Julien seemed to want to do, I persisted. Sooner or later, I would have to find a way to break the awful silence between us. But how?

Julien, I'm sorry. . . . No.

Julien, I need to apologize. . . . No.

Julien, there's something I need to tell you. . . . Definitely not. I played distractedly, trying to think of how to start a real conversation with him. *No wonder he keeps winning,* I thought bitterly. *My mind is a million miles away.*

"Another round?"

I looked down to see that Julien had won again. In response, I blurted out, "Do you, um, want to talk about anything?"

"Nope. I'll deal this time."

"Look, Julien—"

"I told you, I don't want to talk about it, Sara!" he snapped.

That shut me up. I studied my cards, determined to drop the subject like a hot potato. He didn't want to talk about it? Fine! We wouldn't talk about it.

"I just . . . I hate that you saw me get beat up like that. It's so humiliating," said Julien. His eyes stayed hidden behind his cards. His voice, however, ventured over the top of his hand. "I'm so tired of being seen as this weak, pathetic little creature. The crab. Before I got polio, I used to run so fast, Sara. I was the fastest kid in my class."

You're still fast, even on your crutches, when you want to be, I was tempted to say. But I remembered something Mademoiselle Petitjean used to say to us in class. "You have two ears but only one mouth for a reason. Try to listen more than you speak." This seemed like a listening moment, for sure.

"And the thing is," continued Julien, "I still remember what that felt like. I know I'll never run like that again, but that doesn't make me weak, or pathetic, which is how people see me."

I shook my head, unable to keep silent any longer. "I don't see you like that," I told him. "I see you as being really brave."

Julien made a face. "Ugh! That's even worse! You think I'm brave because I walk with crutches?" He looked at me like I was being stupid. "Crutches don't make me brave! They make me able to get around!"

I cringed. Leave it to me to open my mouth and make things worse. "Yes, of course. I'm sorry, Julien."

"You just don't get it," he said dismissively.

"No, I do! I get it all!" I felt an urgent need to make him see that while I wasn't perfect—and I knew it!—I also wasn't the enemy. "And you're right. I've been so selfish. I am self-absorbed. And childish. I never stood up for you when people were mean to you in school."

"No, no, Sara. Please, stop. You don't need to apologize."

"But I want to!" I insisted. "I'm sorry that I used to be like the rest of them! I'm sorry I didn't know your name. That I didn't even realize you had a name." I was crying now. I couldn't help it. Nothing mattered if I couldn't show Julien how much it hurt me to know that I had hurt him.

"Sara, it's okay. Really," Julien said. He had put the cards down, and he reached for my hands. "Look, I'm sorry I said those things. You're the best friend I've ever had. The truth is, it doesn't matter how you used to be. It only matters how you are now."

I nodded and tried to say something, but it came out in kind of a snuffly snort, which made both of us laugh. Julien unrolled his shirtsleeve and offered it to me. I used it to wipe my eyes but couldn't bring myself to blow my nose on it.

"The other day with Vincent," he continued, "you were willing to risk your life just to save mine. No one's ever done that for me before. I should be thanking you. That was really brave of you."

"It was?" That honestly hadn't occurred to me. "Look, when I say I think you're brave, it's not because of your crutches. It's because of how you stood up to them. It's because of everything you're risking to help me."

"Aww. Well, if you put it that way, okay, I'll accept your compliment."

I smiled and used my own sleeve to blow my nose. Loudly.

Julien laughed. "Anyway, how about we go back to the way things used to be?"

"Okay, I'd like that."

Julien picked up his cards and grabbed my hand of cards as well. Reshuffling the deck, he said, "So if we're going to start over, let's really start over. You deal this round."

"All right," I said. "Prepare to take a beating!" As soon as the words left my mouth, I cringed. "Sorry! I didn't mean it like that!"

"Oh, no, I can take it," he assured me. "But I don't think the one who just lost six rounds should be making idle threats."

"Five!" I corrected him.

"Going to be six soon," he said confidently.

"We'll see," I said, dealing the cards. This time I was able to pay attention to the game. To study my cards. To choose my moves strategically. Which, I told myself as I set another card down, *was going to make the difference this ti*—

"Ha ha! I win again!" teased Julien.

I groaned with frustration. "How is that possible? How do you always win? I can beat your mother, so why can't I ever beat you?"

"I suppose I get my card-playing skills from my papa."

"He must be so proud," I joked. "However, just once I'd like to win."

"You're suggesting I should let you win?" Julien raised an eyebrow.

"No! I'm just saying— Forget it, let's play again. One more game. Okay?"

"For you? Anything," he said.

PART THREE

But the enemy came like thunder in the wood. . . .
—Muriel Rukeyser, "Seventh Elegy: The Dream-Singing Elegy"

"Can you teach me to play belote?" asked Julian.

"Of course," replied Grandmère with a smile. "But if you expect to be able to beat me, I have some disappointing news. There came a time when I began to win at belote."

"No way."

She nodded proudly. "It drove Julien crazy, especially when I teased him about no longer being the undefeated champion." Grandmère sighed. "It was such a strange time. And it went on for so long. That first month seemed like an eternity, and the ones that followed also felt like they went on forever. At a certain point I realized that I had been living in that hayloft for over a year."

"A year?" Julian looked shocked. "Without ever going outside, or sleeping in a real bed, or using an actual toilet?"

"What choice did I have? It wasn't all bad. Despite my limited circumstances, every day was not identical to the one before it. Though some days were nearly unbearable. Imagine living in an unheated barn in the dead of winter, with the icy wind whipping through the holes in the walls. There were nights when I would lie awake shivering, praying for the morning to come. You think summer in the city can be hot? Try living in a grimy old barn—all that dusty hay and stagnant air. Sometimes it got so bad, I could barely breathe."

"Right, so . . . how did you deal with all that?"

His grandmother shrugged. "My dear boy, you can get used to anything. That is a trick of human nature. We get used to things. I know it might be hard to imagine, but your très chic grandmère stopped caring so much about her looks. As I grew taller and skinnier, my daily outfit was one of Jean-Paul's old work shirts and a hand-me-down pair of his pants."

"That must have been quite a look with your fancy red shoes," joked Julian.

"Oh, by then I had outgrown those red shoes, in more ways than one." Grandmère laughed at the memory. "Besides, they ended up serving a far more practical purpose."

CHAPTER ONE
Spring 1944

"Shoo! Git! Come on, shoo!" I yelled threateningly, waving a red shoe at a tiny mouse skittering back into the haystack. No sooner had it disappeared from view than out of the corner of my eye, I saw another small gray form dart out. "Oh no you don't!" I cried, chasing the second mouse and nearly flattening its tail with a thud of my shoe. "Take that! And that!" I added, whacking the floor repeatedly for good measure.

"Sara? What in the world is going on up there?"

I froze, hands in the air with red shoes on them like gloves.

"Nothing," I said guiltily. Though in all honesty I felt entitled to establish some rules for my fellow hayloft dwellers. I didn't want to hurt the mice, truly. But I lost my patience with them when they darted across my face in the night and made a beeline for everything I ate.

Julien tossed me his crutches and pulled himself up. He had done it so many times, and he was so much taller and stronger now, that this was one swift move rather than a series of awkward ones.

"Terrorizing the poor little rodents again?" he asked. "You're turning into a regular Mouse-olini, aren't you?"

"I am not," I retorted. "Besides, they started it."

He looked amused. "Oh, really?"

I gathered up a handful of my hair like a ponytail and showed him the ends to prove it. "You see? They nibble on it while I sleep!"

"You lucky girl," he replied. "Monsieur Souris is a famous hairdresser. All the ladies in Paris line up for him to trim their locks. And here he is, giving you haircuts for free!"

"I do need a haircut," I admitted after giving him a light swat for teasing me. "A real one, that is!"

"I'll see if Maman can take care of it. And I am sorry about the mice."

"It's okay. It's just . . ." I sighed. "I feel like I could put up with them, and with everything, a lot better if I knew when it was going to end."

"I know," he said, sitting down at the table with me. "I wish I could bring you some good news. Oh, wait, I do have one piece of news. We have a new directeur at school. Guess why!"

"Pastor Luc joined a traveling circus?"

"Actually, I heard he joined the Resistance. He's apparently part of the Maquis now. And I heard that thousands of maquisards are gathering in the mountains, preparing for an assault on the Germans."

"That's incredible!" I said. I tried to imagine our gentle, soft-spoken principal training to be a Resistance fighter. And

I wondered if what Vivienne had said to him had moved him to volunteer.

"It's a good sign," agreed Julien. "There were two major attacks in German cities recently—it's been all over the news. So maybe the war will end soon?"

"I hope." It was such a funny word, "hope." I still said it often, and I pictured hope as a candle that needed to keep burning, no matter what. But for me the flame had been just about extinguished. I had nearly lost hope of ever seeing my home and my family again.

"Speaking of joining up, you know what else I heard?" asked Julien. "Vincent quit school, and people are saying that he joined the Milice."

I let out a low whistle. "Like father, like son, I suppose."

"Exactly," said Julien. "The Nazi doesn't fall far from the tree."

"Is it just a rumor, or is it true?" I asked.

"I'm pretty sure it's true. What, you're surprised?"

"Of course not! I know he's a monster. But for some reason I still hope"—there was that word again—"that people can change."

"People can," said Julien softly. "But Vincent just might be too far gone already. Can't you see him marching around with those arrogant Milice guys?"

"I can imagine," I reminded him.

"Sorry—I always forget that you don't get to see everything I do! Though you should be glad." He made a face. "The Milice are the worst. Because they're French, like us. But they're like honorary Nazis."

"Like the *gendarmes*?"

He shook his head. "No, the *gendarmes* were regular policemen before the Nazis came along. The Milice is a new police unit full of guys like Vincent who always wanted to have free rein to be thugs."

I shuddered at the thought. "Wow. Maybe I don't want to go outside after all," I said.

"I mean, it's not perfect up here. But there are some advantages. You get to spend time with me, and of course there are the amenities. Like free haircuts." He took hold of a lock of my hair and pretended to nibble on it.

I laughed and pulled back, so my hair slipped through his fingers. "Some advantages!" I complained. But I could feel his eyes on me, and I could feel myself enjoying his attention.

I wondered if any of the girls at school had noticed how he'd changed in the past year. It wasn't just that he was more self-confident, more open, and quicker to laugh. He had also filled out and gotten more handsome. I wouldn't have been surprised if Mariann or Sophie had had crushes on him—that is, if they could see past his crutches and the ridiculous rumors about his smell.

A wave of jealousy at the very thought of one of my friends flirting with Julien took me by surprise. I pushed it away and tried to reassure myself. They probably hadn't noticed his dimples and warm brown eyes like I had. There were times he would catch me staring at him, and I'd have to turn away. And when I'd find him looking at me and he'd blush, I'd dare to think that maybe he felt the same way about me.

Increasingly, I daydreamed about the two of us. There was a movie I saw, back when I lived in Aubervilliers-aux-Bois and I was nine or ten, in which a beautiful woman fainted and a strong, handsome man caught her and carried her to a sofa. I thought about that scene often. If something like that happened, I wasn't sure if Julien could carry me, on account of his crutches. But I kept picturing myself in his arms like the lady in the film.

"Sara?"

"Huh?" I blinked, realizing that Julien had caught me daydreaming again.

"I asked if you wanted to go for a drive," said Julien.

"Oh. Of course," I said, happy that, at least on this occasion, his mind-reading skills didn't seem to be revealing my secrets. "Can I drive?" I asked.

"What? Why should you drive?" he asked, getting up and tossing his crutches down below.

"Well, I'm older," I reminded him.

"Barely. And I'm taller," he said proudly, sliding off the edge of the hayloft. This was a recent development, and one he liked to point out.

"Barely!" I replied, following him.

Then, one evening in May, Julien and I were up in the hayloft, sitting back to back, as we often did. We had gotten into the habit of connecting to each other physically in the most casual of ways. If we weren't back to back, we were side by side. Even when we played cards, we often had our feet or knees touching. I'm not sure when this started, and we never said a word about it. It just sort of developed, and I liked it.

Out of the blue, he said, "Hey, Sara. I have a surprise for you."

"A surprise?" I asked. "You mean, like a treasure?" I had told him about the thoughtful little presents my father used to bring home to me when he traveled.

He laughed. "It's not from a store, if that's what you mean."

"Some of the best things aren't," I pointed out.

"Close your eyes," he said. I felt him twist around and put something gently in my hands. "Okay, you can open them."

I looked down. "It's a little bird," I said with delight. I held it up to examine it more closely. It was carved from a single piece of wood, with carefully detailed features and even tiny feather notches on its wings. It was a deep chestnut color, polished smooth. It fit perfectly into the curve of my hand.

"Do you like it?" Julien asked. "I whittled it for you."

"It's lovely," I told him. "Thank you."

"Were you really surprised? I could have sworn you saw me working on it."

"I didn't," I told him. It was sort of true. I had seen him working on something and secretly hoped it was for me. "I love it," I said, turning around so now I was sitting on the floor facing him. My heart was beating fast and I felt certain that

Julien's was, too. I leaned a little forward, my hands holding the bird between us. I took a deep breath. "I love . . ."

"Yes," said Julien, leaning in as well.

Creeak . . .

By now, I knew the unmistakable sound of the barn door opening.

"Wait. Did you hear that?" I whispered, hoping it might be the wind.

"Happy birthday to you, happy birthday to you."

Julien's eyes sparkled as I got to my feet and ran to the edge of the hayloft. There were Vivienne and Jean-Paul, serenading me while holding the most beautiful cake.

"Happy birthday, dear Sara," Julien chimed in. "Happy birthday to you."

"Wait. It's May twenty-eighth?" I asked, feeling ridiculous. "How did I forget my own birthday?"

"I don't know, but it's a good thing you have us," he replied. "We didn't forget!"

"It is a good thing," I agreed.

Julien accepted the cake and a variety of other provisions from his mother before helping his parents climb up to join us. Then, balancing on his crutches, he extended his arm to me, like a prince in a fairy tale. Together we made our way to the table, where Vivienne presented me with my cake. A whole cake! With luscious dark brown icing all over and the deep mouthwatering scent of—

"Chocolate? Is it really chocolate?" I asked greedily.

Vivienne laughed. "Yes!" she said proudly.

"Vivienne has been saving our ration points for months," Jean-Paul told me. "Once she gets an idea into her head, good luck trying to stand in her way."

"That was so kind of you!" I told her. "I hope it hasn't been too hard—"

"Hurry up, Sara!" interrupted Julien. "Finish cutting already! Cake first, conversation second."

"Yes, sir!" I sliced four thick pieces and we all dug in.

Mmmmmm . . . As I happily shoveled cake into my mouth, I had a fleeting moment of missing Papa and, especially, Maman. I often pictured them hovering above me, between my head and the rafters where the bats lived. Maman was gazing at me with love but also cringing at my shocking lack of table manners. *Please forgive me, Maman! If I make it through this war alive, I'll go back to using my best manners,* I promised her.

And I'll eat chocolate every single day for the rest of my life, I promised myself.

I looked over at Vivienne and noticed she was surreptitiously licking her fork.

Julien must have seen her, because he soon followed suit.

Then Jean-Paul.

Finally, I took mine and timidly began to do the same.

The Beaumiers all started laughing. "Oh, Sara, you must think us such rubes," said Vivienne.

"Not at all!" I told her. "Remember, I have been living in a hayloft for over a year. If you told me fork licking was the latest trend in high society, I would have to believe you."

"It is!" cried Julien. "Everyone who's anyone is doing it!"

"They'd have to be fools not to," I said. "I still can't believe you were able to make me a chocolate birthday cake! How many ration points did that take?"

"And how did you find chocolate?" asked Jean-Paul. "There's been none in the shops for months."

"Oh, mon Dieu!" exclaimed Vivienne. "Don't make me reveal all my secrets. Besides, it was worth it. Oh, wait, I almost forgot—I brought milk to go with the cake. Who'd like some?"

My hand shot up, as did Jean-Paul's. Julien raised both of his at once, making everyone laugh.

But the mention of milk made me remember something. "Wait, how did you get past the Lafleurs tonight?"

Vivienne made a strange face, like our neighbor's cat Louis when our other neighbor's parakeet went missing. I looked at Jean-Paul, and his mustache was twitching at the corners, as if he was trying hard not to laugh. One glance at Julien made it clear that whatever was going on, he was in on it, too.

"We did something naughty . . . ," Vivienne finally confessed. "God forgive us."

"They'll be fine," said Jean-Paul. "Well rested and none the wiser."

"I'll drink to that," joked Julien.

"What are you talking about?" I asked.

The three Beaumiers exchanged glances. Then Jean-Paul piped up. "Well, last week I had my tooth pulled, and the doctor gave me sleeping powder for the pain. I had a little extra, and . . ."

"And I put it in the Lafleurs' milk this afternoon," boasted Julien, grinning.

"Sleeping powder! Did it work?" I asked.

"Did it ever!" replied Julien. "We could hear them snoring through the walls!"

"All right, all right," said Vivienne. "Enough drama for one night. We have one more surprise. Our evening entertainment continues with . . . the evening news!"

"The news?" I gasped as Vivienne pulled their utility radio out of her market bag. Jean-Paul switched it on and turned the dial, trying to tune in a clear signal.

Static . . . more static . . . and then . . .

". . . by the Allies . . ."

"I think that's Radio London," Julien told me.

"Shhh!" came from both of his parents. We all leaned in, staring at the radio. My stomach might have been full of cake, but the rest of me was hungry for news.

"I repeat," said the radio announcer. "More developments in the wake of Monte Cassino's liberation by the Allies ten days ago. The German First Parachute Division has been destroyed."

"Destroyed?" I said with wonder.

Jean-Paul nodded solemnly. "I had heard rumors that the Allies were closing in. Hopefully, France will be next."

"Do you really think so?" I asked. I was terrified to get my hopes up, but hearing Jean-Paul say it made it feel possible.

"I believe—"

He started to reply, but stopped speaking as soon as the announcer continued.

"To the southwest of Monte Cassino, the French Expeditionary Corps has taken control of—"

Jean-Paul pointed excitedly at the radio. "It's happening all around us. We're gaining strength. I believe the war will be over soon."

"The war will be over soon?" I repeated. I liked those words so much, words I hadn't dared to say in my entire time in hiding. So I said them again. "The war will be over soon."

"The war will be over soon," echoed Julien.

Then his mother stood up, and she too said, "The war will be over soon."

It felt so good, all of us saying it together and having it not be a dream. Perhaps I was giddy from the unexpected party and all that chocolate and sugar, but I couldn't stop smiling.

"The war will be over soon! The war will be over soon!" Julien clapped out a beat, as if we were singing a song, and we all started embracing happily. First Vivienne hugged Jean-Paul. Then I hugged Vivienne and Jean-Paul. And then I reached out and spontaneously hugged Julien. He hugged me back, and I remembered the first time I had hugged him, when he returned my sketchbook to me. All those days of sitting side by side and back to back, but always with a certain careful reserve. And now here we were, finally able to be a little less careful. To revel in a little glimmer of joy and hopefulness after so long. I savored the feeling of his arms around me, not wanting to let go of this moment or of him.

But suddenly I remembered that Vivienne and Jean-Paul were standing right there, watching us. I pulled back, and a wave of uncharacteristic awkwardness washed over me. I snuck a peek at Julien, and he seemed to be experiencing the same thing. His face was flushed, perhaps with the excitement of the news, but I sensed that he too was feeling something more.

"Uh . . . um, here, Vivienne, let me help you with that."

Quickly, I busied myself with collecting and stacking the dishes. Vivienne packed away the utility radio, the milk bottle, and everything else she had brought in her market bags, and I bade the whole Beaumier family a fond and grateful farewell.

"*Bonne nuit! Fais de beaux rêves!*" called Vivienne softly from the barn door.

I waved from the hayloft before trying to settle in for the night.

I lay down on my mattress.

I pulled my blanket around me.

I stared up at the rafters.

How can I sleep at a time like this??

Blame it on the chocolate cake. Blame it on the radio broadcast. Or blame it on the real culprit: that hug. I was hopelessly smitten—by Julien, and by the exciting prospect of returning to the world and all its pleasures and possibilities.

I closed my eyes and tried to sleep, but instead of drifting off into my dreams, I lay there imagining leaving the barn. *The war will soon be over,* I thought, *and then what? What would I do? Where would I go?*

First, you'll fly home to me, I pictured Papa saying. I ran into his arms and rested my head on his chest. He looked the same to me, of course, and I could tell how happy he was to see that while we'd been apart, I had grown from a little girl into a strong young woman. *And me*, Maman would say, coming over to wrap both of us in her loving embrace. I lay there with my eyes closed, grinning like an idiot. In all my time in the barn, I had not dared to picture our family's tender reunion—without the chance of it actually happening, I knew it would hurt too much to wish for it.

"Aughhh!" I sat up abruptly and swatted wildly at a mouse that had dashed by my ear.

Squeeeak!

"You're lucky I don't sleep with my shoes!" I called after it. But I was feeling too good to bother chasing it down. *Fine*, I thought, *the mice can find some cake crumbs. They also deserve to celebrate that the war will soon be over.*

Since I didn't feel sleepy in the least, I got up and decided to draw for a while. I pulled out my sketchbook and selected a pencil—Julien had recently sharpened several for me. But when I went to draw a picture, I started to write instead.

Mrs. Julien Beaumier, I wrote boldly. I admired it before quickly scribbling it out. Not quite yet. But maybe, someday.

In my head, I heard Papa clear his throat.

So many things to do first, he reminded me. *You're a clever girl. You should get yourself a degree, like your mother!*

"Yes, Papa," I said dutifully. In my sketchbook, I wrote: Go to a university. To study—

Science, suggested Papa.

Or math, Maman chimed in.

—art, I wrote.

Papa and Maman frowned.

Art and design. Fashion design. Art history, I added. I will follow my passion and work hard and make Papa and Maman proud.

It's hard to argue with that, Maman whispered to Papa.

I kept writing. Julien will go to a university, too, I wrote. He'll study mathematics, of course. We'll study together and stay great friends. On the weekends, we'll go on picnics and go to cafés and go to see movies. He'll take me out in a rowboat, just for fun. And we'll go for drives in a real working car with actual inflated tires. Someday maybe we'll even go on an actual trip to Africa, not just in our imaginations. We'll take long walks and hold hands and talk about the future. We'll start a life together.

I wrote and wrote, losing all track of the passage of time. I wrote about so many things, but mostly about Julien. It felt good to be finally able to put my feelings for him somewhere. And once I started putting my feelings into words, it was like a water spigot stuck in the on position! I filled pages and pages with my feelings for Julien. Then I shifted into drawing mode and balanced out my pages of words with pages of images of Julien and hearts and feathers and swirling designs that flowed as freely as my love for him. Because that's what I had come to realize was what I was feeling. Love for Julien.

The sound of something hitting the ground startled me. I looked and saw that it was my pencil. I yawned, stretched, and picked it up. Then I closed my sketchbook and put it away for the night.

I had just gotten back into bed when I heard a small noise downstairs.

Grandmère (Helen Mirren, left) sits and talks about her childhood in France with her grandson, Julian (Bryce Gheisar, right).

Julian (Bryce Gheisar) tries to find a group of friends to fit in with at his new school.

Sara (Ariella Glaser) smiles as she walks her bicycle into the schoolyard.

Julien (Orlando Schwerdt, center) returns a dropped sketchbook
to Sara (Ariella Glaser, right) as her friends look on.

Sara (Ariella Glaser, center) and her friends Mariann (Selma Kaymakci, left) and Sophie (Mia Kadlecova, right) laugh as they run down the street together.

Rose (Olivia Ross, left) and Max (Ishai Golan, right) explain to their daughter, Sara (Ariella Glaser, center), that they will have to flee their home.

Sara (Ariella Glaser, center) and her fellow Jewish classmates hide in an alcove as they plan their escape from the German soldiers.

Sara (Ariella Glaser) huddles in the hayloft of the drafty barn as she waits for Julien and his parents to return.

Sara (Ariella Glaser) draws a scene in her sketchbook
by candlelight as she hides in the barn.

Sara (Ariella Glaser, right) and Julien (Orlando Schwerdt, left)
pretend to drive the Beaumiers' car down the grand streets of Paris.

Julien (Orlando Schwerdt, left) walks through the schoolyard as Vincent (Jem Matthews, leftmost of the three boys) and his friends mock him.

Vincent (Jem Matthews) enters the Beaumiers' barn, suspicious that someone is hiding within.

Julien (Orlando Schwerdt, left) gazes at Sara (Ariella Glaser, right) during a rare moment out of the barn to see the bluebells in the forest.

Vivienne (Gillian Anderson) watches from the doorway of her home.

Sara (Ariella Glaser) rushes to inform Vivienne (Gillian Anderson) of some terrible news about Julien.

Grandmère (Helen Mirren) gazes skyward toward a white bird as she leaves the exhibition of her artwork.

"Really, mice?" I muttered.

Then I heard it again, and I realized that whatever it was, it was too big to be a mouse. I tiptoed over to the edge of the hayloft and looked down.

"Julien? What are you doing here? What time is it?"

"I'm not sure," he said. "Maybe midnight, I guess. I'm sorry—did I wake you?"

I shook my head. "I can't sleep," I admitted.

"Good!" he replied. "Can you come down?"

I hesitated. "I'm in my nightgown," I told him. It was Vivienne's hand-me-down nightgown, and it was the perfect weight for spring nights in the barn. Provided I was under my blanket, that is—the night air itself had quite a chill, even in spring.

"Put on your sweater," Julien directed. "And shoes. I'll explain when you come down."

You mean boots, I thought. My pretty red shoes were mouse-shooing devices now. Not to mention they were no longer pretty and no longer fit. The soles of my feet had gotten tough from all the time I spent barefoot, but the Beaumiers had given me a pair of hand-me-down work boots to protect my feet from the cold and the errant nails on the barn floor.

"Okay, hang on," I said, pulling on my cardigan and yanking on my boots. Back home, I would have called them clod-hoppers. In my new life, the way they looked didn't so much as cross my mind. I put them on without a moment's hesitation. All I thought was Why do I need a sweater and boots to come down? Had Julien invented some new sort of variation on the magic flying chariot game? And why couldn't it wait until the next day—not that I was complaining!

I lowered myself down from the hayloft.

"Okay, here I am."

"Great—are you ready? Let's go."

"Go? What are talking about?" I asked.

"We are going for a walk . . . in the woods," he said.

I stared at him. "Are you crazy?" I asked. "What about the Lafleurs?"

"That sleeping powder is powerful stuff," he assured me. "Just now, when I snuck out, I could still hear them snoring through the walls."

"But what if they wake up?" I wrapped my arms around myself, even though the sweater kept me warm enough. I felt nervous—not just about the Lafleurs, but for many reasons. Who knew what awful things could be waiting for us outside? Spies, Nazis, wolves . . . they all lurked in the dark, and these monsters were real, not the stuff of a young girl's imagination.

Julien put a hand on my arm and looked into my eyes. "Trust me, Sara," he said. "It's safe. I wouldn't suggest it otherwise. We won't be out for long, I promise. But this may be our only chance for a while. And I want you to see something."

I took a deep breath.

"Are you sure about this?" I asked. I meant: about our safety. But I also meant: about us. I felt like his response would tell me everything I needed to know about our future together.

"Trust me," he said. "It will be worth it."

And so Julien held the barn door open. I took a tentative

step forward. Then I did the thing I had been dreaming of for more than a year: I walked out of the barn.

"It was such a magical night." Grandmère took a sip of her wine, letting the memory wash over her.

"I'll bet," said Julian. "I still can't believe you went a whole year without chocolate! Isn't your motto 'One should never go a day without chocolate'?"

"C'est vrai," she replied, smiling. "To this day, it was the most delicious cake I've ever eaten in my life!"

"So, okay, after you left the barn, what happened? What did Julien want you to see?"

"Nothing. Who remembers such things? The moon, probably." She smiled.

"Grandmère," said Julian sternly.

"What?"

"You said you would tell me the whole story."

His grandmother sighed. "I suppose I did. Let's see now, where was I?"

" 'It was such a magical night . . . ,' " Julian prompted.

"It was," she agreed.

CHAPTER TWO

The moon was out, thank goodness, since it was the middle of the night. Julien and I slipped around the side of the barn, and he led the way down the path into the woods.

"Come on, slowpoke," he teased, because I was so distracted by, well, everything. The chill breeze on my face, the sounds of the insects, the silhouettes of the trees swaying . . . it had all been right there, but I hadn't been with any of it, out in the world, in so long. I wanted to linger, to just stop time and drink it all in, but Julien was urging me forward toward whatever it was he wanted me to see. What could possibly be so important? I wondered. But all the same I tried my best to catch up and keep pace.

I stuck my hands in my sweater pockets to keep them warm and was surprised to find something in one of them. I pulled it out and discovered it was the carved bird Julien had made for me. I clutched it in my fist as we stumbled along, massaging its little wooden body to calm my nerves.

The path was dark and—I'll admit it—a little scary. Having

Julien there with me helped, though a few times I tripped over roots and nearly knocked him down in the dark. We tried to keep quiet, just in case we came across anyone else using the path. But thankfully, we saw no one. Julien took me deeper into the forest, and I started to worry that we might not be able to find our way back out.

"Julien, do you—"

"Shhhh," he replied, then whispered, "We're almost there. Look."

I turned to see where he was pointing. I could barely make it out, but my jaw dropped at the bizarre and yet familiar sight.

"Bluebells!" I cried.

Julien nodded. "I stumbled upon them a few weeks ago, when they were just starting to bloom, and I remembered your story. I figured if they kept going, they might be at their peak right about now. I was planning to pick some and bring them to you, but tonight I realized I could give you something even better."

"You have no idea what this means to me," I told him. It was like stepping into a memory and a dream all in one. The forest floor was literally sparkling in the moonlight, every flower petal glowing magically. "It's . . . perfect."

"I'm glad," said Julien, smiling shyly.

Together, we walked around the glade.

"When I got home, I couldn't fall asleep," Julien confided in me. "I was so happy."

"Me too," I said. "I can't believe the end of the war is in sight."

"Yeah," said Julien. "It's not just that, though. It's feeling like . . ."

His voice trailed off, and I turned and looked at him. As the moonlight reflected in his eyes, I finished his thought. ". . . like we can dream again," I said.

"Exactly!" We were standing face to face, and—

Hooo! Hooo!

The owl's cry startled me, and I grabbed for Julien's hands. I thought about letting go once I realized there was no danger. But I didn't, and neither did he.

"And I just want you to know," he continued, his eyes locked on mine, "that . . . in the future I dream for myself . . . um, well, I just want you to know . . . you're always part of it." He swallowed and looked down, as if he had been concentrating so hard on his words that he had just realized we were holding hands. "You probably know I've always had a crush on you," he said.

Lub-dub, lub-dub, lub-dub. Had my heart always been this loud? Or was I suddenly suffering from some strange new condition?

"And I'm wondering," he continued, "do you think, after the war, we—"

"Yes," I said.

Julien smiled. "Yes? I haven't even asked the question yet."

"But I know the answer," I said boldly. The truth was, I had a hunch. But also, "Yes" was my answer no matter what question he might have been asking. "Yes," I repeated.

And then I closed my eyes, leaned forward, and hoped I had guessed correctly.

His lips softly touched mine. I felt a rush of relief—Hallelujah, I *was* right!—and a burst of excitement. I was kissing Julien! He was kissing me! We were kissing each other! Right now, standing in a field of blooming bluebells, the magical fairy garden of my dreams! It was better than fainting and being carried. It was even better than chocolate cake. It was still going on, and I hoped it would never end.

It was just one kiss.

One very long kiss.

One very long and wonderful kiss.

We walked back to the barn hand in hand. We talked, but so many things had happened in twenty-four hours that I probably babbled like a fool. If I did, Julien was too sweet to point out that I wasn't making any sense. All I could think was Julien! And I! Just! Kissed!!!

"So, here we are," said Julien after we slipped back into the barn. This time we went through the hole in the back wall, just in case the Lafleurs had woken up from their unexpected nap.

"Here we are," I echoed.

He smiled and squeezed my hand. "Good night, Sara," he said.

"No, wait!" On the walk back, something had occurred to me. Julien had given me so much—his gifts for my birthday, of course, but so much more—and I wanted to give him something special in return. But what? I had nothing to give. All I had in the world was his family's used clothing, some random pieces of secondhand furniture, and a pile of dog-eared old books.

And, I suddenly realized, one more thing.

I pulled myself up to the hayloft, rummaged around, and returned carrying a package.

"Close your eyes and hold out your hands," I told Julien, happy to finally be able to reverse our roles. "No peeking."

"Says the queen of peeking," he teased. But he did as I asked.

I placed the parcel in his hands. I had quickly wrapped it in one of his father's old work shirts.

"Okay, you can look now."

Julien opened his eyes. He looked amused at my wrapping job and carefully peeled back the fabric.

"Your sketchbook?" he asked. "Really?"

I nodded happily. I couldn't wait for him to look through it and discover that I'd filled every page with pictures and words, many of which were inspired by him. I had poured my heart into my sketchbook, so it brought me joy to give it to Julien.

He hugged it to his chest. "I'll treasure it forever."

"Just like I'll treasure my little bird," I told him, pulling it out of my sweater pocket and stroking its carved feathers.

"Well, I guess I should probably go home and try to get some sleep," he said.

"Yeah, me too. Wait for me to climb up?"

"Of course."

He watched as I pulled myself up to my perch.

"Good night, ma chérie," he called.

"Good night, Julien," I replied.

As I waved goodbye from the loft, he removed his cap and gave me a little salute.

"Vive l'humanité!" he called. Then he slipped out of the barn.

I got into bed, still wearing my sweater. There was no way I could possibly sleep after all that excitement, yet my eyelids felt heavy, so I closed them. I soon noticed that my mattress had melted away and I was once again walking peacefully in the forest among the bluebells. I looked around for Julien, but before I could find him, a little bird flew down and landed on my shoulder.

"Hello," I said to it. "Have you seen Julien?"

"We will take you to him," the bird answered.

"We?" I asked.

Just then I noticed another small white bird. And another. And another. Until the sky was dense with them. I had never seen anything like it—a flock of white birds, swooping down from the sky. But for some reason, I wasn't afraid. I knew I could trust them.

So I let them surround me.

And I felt them gently lift me up.

And the next thing I knew, I was flying.

"I can't believe I'm talking with my grandmother about kissing," said Julian.

"Pourquoi pas?" Grandmère asked, raising an eyebrow. "Kissing is nothing to be ashamed of."

"I know, but . . . I dunno. You're my grandmother. It feels a little weird."

"It was not weird," she told him. "It was wonderful. I will remember that kiss forever."

"Okay!" said Julian, embarrassed. He cleared his throat and attempted to change the subject. "Did you ever regret giving him your sketchbook?" he asked.

"Oh yes," she replied quietly. "But not for the reasons you're probably thinking."

CHAPTER THREE

I woke up the next morning with a start. Bright sunlight was seeping through the cracks in the walls and window boards, indicating that it was later than my usual wake-up time. I used my bucket, poured a little fresh water into my basin, and rinsed my hands and face. Next, I went to look for my sketchbook and could not find it. It was only then that I remembered where it had gone.

Julien has my sketchbook, I realized with concern. Certainly, it had plenty of drawings of birds and flowers in it. But it also had pages and pages of my romantic ramblings, documenting my growing obsession with a certain boy. The boy who now had *those very pages in his hands.*

Julien has my sketchbook! was my next thought. Because the truth of the matter was, I secretly wanted him to read them, even when I wrote them. And especially now that I had confirmed that his feelings for me were every bit as strong and as deep as mine.

I pictured him sitting at the breakfast table, reading the words from my diary entry after the surprise birthday party:

Such a beautiful night, with such beautiful people! How blessed am I to have the Beaumiers in my life! Thank you, life, for all your wonders. Thank you for all you have given me. Mostly, the belief I now have that all human beings in this world are somehow connected to each other. Maybe I always knew this, but from my little window inside my little barn, I can actually hear the secrets of the world in the still of the night. I swear there are even times when I can hear the planet spinning! I can hear in the chirping of crickets, the faraway sounds of people talking in cafés. I can hear in the flutter of bat wings, the quickened heartbeats of the maquisards hiding in the mountains. I can hear in the soft cooing of the night owls, my papa, somewhere, calling my name. Funny, I used to be so afraid of the night. But now I see it as my time for listening to the soul of the world telling me its secrets. And tonight it whispers, over and over again like a song: "You love Julien." Yes, I answer, I know. I love Julien.

I could picture a secret little happy smile creeping onto his face as he read these words. Vivienne would probably come in and notice it, too. She'd probably even comment on it.

Bonjour, Julien! You look very bright and cheery this morning, she might say. Any particular reason?

Yes, indeed! Sara is in love with me. And I am in love with her!

I burst out laughing at the very idea. There was no way Julien would do that. He would be very respectful and discreet, I was certain. He'd probably respond with something like *Nope. No reason. I should head out now. Don't want to be late for school. À bientôt, Maman! Arrivederci!*

I pictured him giving his mother a sweet exaggerated *bisou* on the cheek with a loud sound effect: *Mwah!*

Vivienne would probably laugh. She always liked it when he played around or acted silly. *Oh, go on.*

I grinned at the scene I had concocted in my head. I snuggled in under my blanket. It had been a long night, and while I had slept well, I had not slept long enough. I closed my eyes to rest a little. I felt glad I had given Julien the sketchbook. It was like a love note between the two of us, and even though I had not asked him to, I hoped that he would do his best to keep it private.

I opened my eyes suddenly, and the light falling across my face made me realize I must have dozed off. For how long? I wondered. I thought perhaps I had heard a motorcycle outside, backfiring in the street. Or maybe it was the bats, though it was not their active time of day.

Then I heard movement downstairs, which would be Vivienne, obviously. I almost called out her name. But as was our rule, I waited for her to first call out to me.

When she didn't, I wasn't sure what to do. Curiosity got the better of me, so I crawled over to the wall of hay, careful not to make a sound.

I looked through an open space in between the bales of hay. And I saw him.

Vincent.

In his dark green Milice uniform, with a matching dark beret atop his head.

And a sinister black rifle in his hands.

I watched him looking around, his eyes unaccustomed to the darkness in the barn. He squinted, scrutinizing every corner before he silently moved forward. I wished this were just a bad dream, but I was all too keenly aware that I was awake and staring down a real threat. A scream lodged in my throat, and I swallowed it hastily. I was terrified that even that gulp, or my breathing, would give away my location. I held my breath, praying he would leave. If I were downstairs, I would be dead already. But in the hayloft, with the wall of hay, I felt I stood a chance of survival.

That is, until the clouds outside shifted and a ray of strong morning light streamed in between the boards across the window. The bright sunbeam caught his eye, and to my horror he turned to see where it was coming from. The window was behind me, so he looked straight at the spot where I was hiding. I felt like I was onstage in a theater, bathed in the spotlight. That sunbeam felt like a beacon announcing where I was! And I was trapped, unable to move for fear of shifting the hay that was still barely concealing me, and making it worse.

Whether he could actually see me was unclear.

But when he opened his mouth, he made one thing very apparent.

"I know you're up there, Jew girl."

Vincent began to pace, aiming his gun at me.

"Did you and your boyfriend actually think you could out-smart me? That's a riot. Really, really funny." He laughed cru-elly. "I saw him, that gimp. Walking—or rather, hobbling—to school early this morning. He must leave the house at dawn—it takes him so long just to get there at that snail's pace he has! Of course, he didn't get there. Want to know why?"

Was he just filling my head with evil lies to get a response? There was no way to tell, so I said nothing and tried to stay hidden, waiting for him to continue.

"He was stopped by a military vehicle. Not sure which one—it's so hard to keep them all straight, isn't it? Maybe it was the *gendarmes*? Hmm, come to think of it, it could have been the Nazis. Regardless, they were very nice to him!" His voice dripped with sarcasm. "Yes, they asked to see his papers and offered to give him a ride to school. Of course, that clumsy gimp dropped his bag and his hat and even one of those dumb crutches he uses. But I was a gentleman! I was with my Milice unit, yet I went to pick up the things he had dropped. And that's when I found your . . . well, I guess you would call it your bird book."

Oh no. My *sketchbook*? A chill went through me.

But Vincent wasn't done. If anything, he was just warm-ing up.

"At least, that's what I remember being in that book when I saw it last, back at school," he continued. "Birds, birds, and more birds! And my memory is so good, I also remembered the little redheaded girl who drew all those birds. Kind of a pretty girl, actually. For a Jew."

If I could have spit on him, I would have. There was nothing I could do but listen to his awful words as his voice got louder and louder.

"See, I'm not stupid. I started putting two and two together. Jew girl goes missing on the day of the big Jew roundup at school and vanishes without a trace. Gimp boy loves Jew girl enough to do anything for her. And now here's gimp boy limping around carrying Jew girl's notebook. Only there are new drawings and words in it . . . because Jew girl is alive and she's in love with gimp boy? What kind of a sick joke is this?!"

RA-TA-TA-TA-TA-TA-TA-TA!

A frenzy of gunshots rang out, with blasts of light accompanying them, rapid-fire.

Oh my God, I am going to die, I thought. I covered my head instinctively and curled myself up as small as possible. All my muscles tensed as I waited for the pain and bloodshed to come.

RA-TA-TA-TA-TA-TA!

RA-TA-TA!

But something awakened inside me. I heard a tiny little voice in my ear, or in my head, speaking clearly. How dare he! Who is he to take your life? After all you have been through, is it really going to end like this?

I felt a rush of angry energy. Slowly, I slid my hand into my sweater pocket and found my little carved bird. I squeezed my hands into two tight fists, holding the bird in my right one.

You're right! I told the voice in my head. If I am going to die, I will not die cowering in a corner like some terrified little mouse. I will face my tormentor head-on. And I will make him face me.

Slowly, I started to get to my feet.

And that's when the light hit me. Literally—I no longer felt like I was standing in the spotlight; I actually was! But if this wasn't just a dream, how could it be?

I looked up and realized where the light was coming from. Holes, lots of them. When he had fired off all those rounds, Vincent had shot holes through the roof.

I didn't even have time to think. I just saw the holes and thought: Freedom. I started to climb the stacked-up hay bales. I reached the top, then heard a noise behind me. A quick backward glance confirmed my fears. Vincent's beret rose over the edge of the loft, as, grunting, he pulled himself higher.

I turned back to the task at hand and reached above my head to see if any of the holes were big enough to pull myself through. None were, but many had frayed edges of soft, splintered wood. Still clutching my little carved bird in my fist, I began punching at the bullet holes to enlarge them. To my great relief, in a few spots the old wood gave way. I hauled myself through the biggest of the holes, praying that the intact parts of the roof wouldn't crumble under my weight.

Once on the roof, I scrambled to the edge, and hesitated. It was higher than I had expected, and despite the adrenaline coursing through my body, I suddenly felt weak.

The sound of Vincent pulling himself onto the roof behind me urged me forward. The risk of broken bones was one I would have to take. I sat on the roof's edge, lowered myself off as far as I could, and let go. I aimed for some bushes, in the hopes they would cushion my fall.

RA-TA-TA!

Vincent's shots from the roof got me to my feet immediately. I began to run, feeling grateful that my legs apparently still worked. I sprinted for the forest, thinking maybe I could lose him in its dense clusters of trees. I got to a patch of bluebells, perhaps the same ones Julien and I had wandered in the night before, but I didn't stop to admire their beauty. I trampled them in my dash for freedom.

"Stop running!" yelled Vincent. "It's no use!"

I ignored him, cringing as more gunshots rang out.

RA-TA-TA-TA-TA-TA-TA-TA!

RA-TA-TA-TA-TA-TA!

RA-TA-TA-TA-TA-TA!

I couldn't breathe. I ducked behind a massive tree and rested a moment, gasping in terror. How could I possibly escape this horrible fate?

RA-TA-TA-TA-TA-TA!

RA-TA-TA-TA-TA-TA!

I closed my eyes and tried to calm myself down, if only so I could think. I looked up frantically. Could I climb a tree? Impossible—I would be seen and shot. Short of sprouting wings, I had no chance of getting away. The ridiculous thought of sprouting wings took me of course to thoughts of Maman and Papa, and our picnics in this same forest, an eternity before. "Maman, please help me," I whimpered softly.

Click-click-click

The strange noise interrupted my plea. Could it be? Was Vincent actually out of bullets?

I peeked out from behind the tree. Vincent was muttering angrily at his rifle.

You coward, I thought. *Always picking on those smaller than you. Acting tough when you're with your gang or carrying a weapon. But inside, you're nothing. You are weak. And I am strong.*

I took a deep breath and turned to face Vincent. I felt ready to say that to him—and more.

But for some reason, he wasn't looking at me anymore.

He looked pale and . . . frightened? He was staring past me, still clutching his now-useless gun but slowly backing away.

Grrrrr . . .

I heard the sound before I turned and followed Vincent's gaze.

There, in the woods, stood a wolf.

And not just any wolf. A huge, shaggy gray-and-black wolf. With long, sharp teeth and hungry eyes.

I've seen you before, I silently told the wolf. Not on any of my picnics or strolls through the woods, but in my dreams, many times. As the wolf growled at Vincent and stalked forward slowly, it glanced over at me. It was the strangest feeling, almost as if the wolf recognized me, too. Stranger still was the look it gave me.

A look that clearly said, *Stay where you are. I will not hurt you.*

The only thing I dared move was my eyes, following that low, swinging, shaggy tail. It flicked dangerously as the wolf continued to move forward.

Hnnn-hnnn . . . , warned the wolf softly. The hair on the scruff of its neck was up, and the wolf stopped and stood its ground. I had the distinct sense that it was trying to tell Vincent to leave its forest. *Do that now, and there won't be any trouble.*

But Vincent had stopped, too. He and the wolf both stood there, staring each other down. Vincent's eyes flashed in my direction, and I realized he was not going away without what he had come for.

Me.

Suddenly, holding out his useless weapon like a shield, Vincent made a dash toward me. But in that same split second, the wolf let out a deep growl . . .

Grrrrrr . . .

. . . and lunged at him.

I froze in fear, clinging to the tree, while the wolf grabbed Vincent by the throat. It shook him from side to side, like a rag doll. I closed my eyes, but not fast enough. The images replayed themselves in my head: the wolf's snapping jaws, the beast snarling and growling as it mutilated Vincent's handsome face. Vincent shrieked in pain and fear, but the wolf showed him no mercy.

Then it was over. Vincent lay still. And without so much as a glance in my direction, the wolf vanished into the woods as silently as it had appeared.

"Vincent?" I called out softly. I was terrified that he might suddenly lurch to his feet and attack me.

He did not move.

Slowly, I crept out and approached him. I stood a careful

distance away, poised to run if necessary. But as I regarded him, I realized that there was no need. Vincent's chest did not rise and fall. His eyes did not blink. Vincent was dead.

Next to him was his beret and his stupid, awful gun.

And a familiar-looking schoolbag.

I stared at the bag.

Lots of schoolboys have bags like that, I told myself. Maybe it's Vincent's bag. Despite everything he had said in the barn, part of me still hoped it had all been lies intended to scare me.

But Vincent was no longer a schoolboy. Julien said he had quit school to join the Milice.

Nervously, I lifted the schoolbag's flap and looked inside.

The first thing I saw made my stomach lurch.

My sketchbook.

If Vincent had been telling the truth about how he got his hands on my sketchbook, it could mean only one thing.

I gasped in horror. "Julien!"

CHAPTER FOUR

I stumbled through the forest, and when I reached the path back to the barn, I quickened my pace.

All I could think was: Julien. I had to get to Vivienne! I had to tell her about Vincent, and that he had the sketchbook I had given to Julien. This, combined with everything Vincent had bragged about witnessing, strongly suggested that Julien had been arrested—for what, I had no idea, but I had recently heard from the Beaumiers that even non-Jews were being arrested on flimsy pretenses. Vivienne could go to the district headquarters and make inquiries about her son, I reasoned. She could bribe a guard and find out if he was being held. Find a compassionate clerk who might take pity on the poor boy's mother. If I hurried, she could get to him and intervene before it was too late!

The barn appeared and I dodged around it, heading straight for the house the Beaumier family shared with the Lafleurs. I didn't even care if the Lafleurs saw me—this was a matter of life and death. Julien, Julien kept running through my head to the beat of my pounding feet. *Need to get to Julien.*

Vivienne, I was pretty sure, had said that her family lived on the left side of the house. I dashed up and knocked frantically on the Beaumiers' front door.

No one responded.

I banged again, many times, and even tried to open the door but found it was locked. Jean-Paul had probably left for work. But where was Vivienne? I looked up at the sky and tried to gauge the time based on the position of the sun. It seemed too early for Vivienne to have left to go to town and do her marketing. Perhaps she was still sleeping?

Or what if the Nazis had taken her, too?

What if she and Julien were both . . . ?

Stop it! Just stop it! I told myself. I forced myself to take a deep breath and try to think logically, like Maman. Presumably, there was a good explanation for where Vivienne was. And the sooner I found her, the sooner she could rescue Julien.

Since no one was coming to the door, I decided to look for another way to get in. Around the side of the house, I noticed a window that was slightly open. I stood on my tiptoes and opened it wider. As I hoisted myself up and lifted a knee to climb in through the open window, I caught a glimpse of my bare foot and gasped. My feet and calves were covered with cuts I must have gotten while trying to escape and running through the woods.

Distracted by my own bruised and bloodied feet, I

practically fell through the window, landing on the floor and narrowly avoiding knocking over a lamp.

"Vivienne?" I called out.

I picked myself up and hobbled through the house, hoping I was not leaving bloodstains on the Beaumiers' floors.

"Vivienne!" I tried again.

I searched every room—bedrooms, the bathroom, the kitchen—with no success.

"Hello?" I called again and again, feeling increasingly concerned.

Then I heard noises coming from the other side of a big set of double doors. It sounded like voices, and the creaking suggested there was a staircase. Of course! I thought, and I almost laughed at myself. After all those months of hiding, how could it not have occurred to me that Julien might be hiding? Perhaps he'd had another confrontation with Vincent, but he had gotten away and run home. I pictured myself falling into his embrace. I would be so relieved, I wouldn't even scold him for giving me such a fright! And maybe Vivienne was up there with him, hiding, too.

I threw open the double doors and found that indeed there was a staircase, which I started up excitedly. So quickly, in fact, that I almost crashed into two people descending the stairs. Not Julien and his mother, but an old man with a thick beard and an old woman in a green wool suit. The man had a black hat, and both of them carried suitcases. The woman frowned and turned to the man.

"I thought the house was going to be empty, Abe," she said.

I stood there, paralyzed with fear and concern. I had not known the stairwell adjoined the neighbors' half of the house; I never would have gone out to the hallway, up the stairs. But as I stared at the couple I presumed to be Madame Lafleur and her husband, it suddenly dawned on me that they couldn't be.

The man's face was familiar to me.

"Rabbi Bernstein?" I blurted out.

The rabbi looked confused and perhaps afraid—it was hard to tell with his beard. I began babbling to quickly reassure him. "Rabbi, it's me, Sara Blum! Max Blum's daughter."

"Max Blum, the surgeon?" asked the rabbi, incredulous.

"Don't move!" interjected a harsh voice.

Startled, I turned—and found myself staring at another elderly couple. They were standing in the doorway of another set of double doors, directly across from the ones from the Beaumiers' apartment, on the other side of the staircase. Unlike Rabbi Bernstein, though, this man did not hold a suitcase in his hand.

He held a pistol, and he pointed it straight at me.

"No!" cried the rabbi, quickly descending the staircase and holding his free hand out in alarm. "Lafleur, put the gun down. I know this girl. Put the gun away."

Madame Bernstein followed behind. She and her husband bravely planted themselves between the armed man and me.

Gun? Lafleurs? The Bernsteins know the Lafleurs? I looked from face to face, completely mystified. "What is going on?" I asked. "I don't understand."

"There's no time to explain!" snapped the man with the gun, who the rabbi had called Lafleur. "Rabbi, you have to leave now or you won't get another chance. The truck is waiting."

"Please, wait a moment while we figure this out!" pleaded the rabbi. He turned to me. "Sara, why are you here?"

Despite the fact that I had spent months trying to avoid having the Lafleurs find out about my secret hiding place, I could not bring myself to lie to the rabbi. "The Beaumiers have been hiding me in the barn."

"The Beaumiers?" said Monsieur Lafleur dismissively. "The Beaumiers are Nazi collaborators."

"What? No, they're not!" I replied. "In fact, they thought you were!"

Both of the Lafleurs shook their heads, and Monsieur Lafleur lowered his weapon with an apologetic nod in my direction.

"No, Sara," said Rabbi Bernstein, a familiar sparkle returning to his eyes. "The Lafleurs have been hiding us in their attic for almost two years. Today we're being smuggled out by the Armée Juive."

Madame Bernstein nodded at her husband's mention of the Jewish Army. Then she stepped toward me and put a kindly hand on my shoulder.

"Why don't you come with us, dear?" she asked.

I looked into her eyes. She was offering me something I could barely wish for—a chance at freedom. Any other day, I might have jumped at the chance. "I can't," I told her. "I have to tell Vivienne: Julien was arrested today."

"That sweet boy?" said Madame Lafleur, her stern expression transformed into one of concern. "That must be why Vivienne left in such a hurry this morning."

"She did?!" I asked.

Monsieur Lafleur nodded. "Jean-Paul picked her up in a car and they sped away."

He cleared his throat and turned to the Bernsteins. "Listen, Rabbi. If you want any hope of escaping, you have to leave—now."

The Bernsteins hesitated. They looked at each other, then at me.

"We'll take care of the girl until the Beaumiers return," Madame Lafleur assured the Bernsteins. I stared, astonished, as Monsieur Lafleur and the rabbi embraced like brothers.

"Write to us when you get to Jerusalem," said Monsieur Lafleur.

"We will," promised the rabbi. "God will remember your kindness to us, old friend."

I watched from the window as the Bernsteins slipped outside to a truck that had pulled up in front of the house. It was army green and nondescript, with no markings, and in the back were what appeared to be many sacks of produce. The rabbi turned and gave one final wave in our direction.

"Vive l'humanité!" he cried.

"Vive l'humanité!" I heard Monsieur Lafleur whisper, like a prayer.

While the driver idled the engine, another man helped

the Bernsteins onto the back of the truck and arranged empty potato sacks to hide them and their belongings from view.

"How long will it take them to get to Jerusalem?" I asked Madame Lafleur.

"I wish I knew," she replied. "We're told their initial destination will be Trieste, in Italy. If the situation there doesn't get worse, they'll be transported to Palestine next."

Together, we watched the truck pull away. "Come with us," said Madame Lafleur when we could no longer see it. "We can wait for Vivienne upstairs, where the Bernsteins have been living."

Determinedly, she used her cane to climb the stairs, Monsieur Lafleur and I following behind her. In the attic was a basin like the one I used for washing myself in the barn. She filled it with water and set it on the floor, then encouraged me to put my cut-up feet into it.

Then the Lafleurs sat with me, and I told them about my encounter with Vincent.

Monsieur Lafleur winced when I got to the part about Vincent hunting me, in the barn and the woods. "We heard the gunshots," he said. He and his wife exchanged a look. "We thought maybe they had come for us," he added.

I continued my story, recounting how the wolf had appeared out of nowhere and attacked Vincent, killing him. It seemed like something out of a dream, or one of my childhood nightmares, I told them, yet for reasons I could not explain, the wolf left me completely unharmed.

"The wild beasts of the Mernuit are dangerous and unpredictable," said Madame Lafleur in a grave tone of voice. "You are very lucky to be alive, my dear."

I knew she was right. However, I also knew that the most dangerous and unpredictable beast in the forest that day was not a wolf. Feeling considerably more relaxed, I went on to tell them everything that had happened to me since the day of the roundup at school. As I explained about the lengths Vivienne and Julien had gone to in order to avoid being seen by the Lafleurs, they both shook their heads in disbelief.

"To think, this whole time, the Beaumiers were as mistrustful of us as we were of them," said Madame Lafleur. "Every day, she would walk into town!" She shrugged, looking embarrassed. "I assumed she was meeting with the Germans."

"How do you know Rabbi Bernstein?" I asked Monsieur Lafleur.

"We served in the infantry together in the Great War," he replied. As he proudly continued, he seemed to sit a little taller in his chair. "He was like a brother to me. When he needed a place to stay, I did not think twice. Damn the Nazis to hell."

"How are your feet now, chérie?" asked Madame Lafleur, coming over to check on me.

"Oh, they're fine," I told her. "I didn't even realize how cut up they got."

"Sara!"

At the sound of my name, Monsieur Lafleur rose and went to the attic window. He beckoned for me to join him, and when I did, he pointed at the barn.

"It is Vivienne," he told me, though of course I knew from her voice. "She's looking for you in the barn."

I waited at the window for what felt like an eternity until Vivienne finally emerged. She looked drained and hopeless—at least until she looked up and spotted me waving frantically from the attic window. I could see the relief in Vivienne's eyes when she saw me. She had probably imagined the worst.

I stood by the attic door, and eventually Vivienne appeared. Before I could say anything, she grabbed me and held me tight.

"Oh, Sara, thank God," she cried.

I clung to her and she to me. I didn't want to let go, in part because I was so relieved to see her again, but also in part because with every passing minute, I was losing hope for Julien.

Finally I pulled back and faced her. "Vivienne, there's something you need to know. It's about Julien, and—"

As her eyes met mine, I stopped talking. It was clear from her face: she already knew.

Vivienne sat down, looking defeated. She stared off into space and began to explain what she could about the awful events of the morning. "When Jean-Paul arrived at work today, a coworker told him he had seen Julien taken by soldiers."

A lump formed in my throat as Vivienne continued. "Jean-Paul came home and picked me up. We drove first to the Kommandantur, but they knew of no arrests that morning. Then we drove to the Milice headquarters, but they told us nothing. Not only that—they laughed at us."

"Barbarians," muttered Madame Lafleur.

Vivienne nodded. "But as we were leaving, one officer told us they had arrested some hospital patients this morning. Jean-Paul went to see what he could find there. I came back to check on Sara." She sighed and leaned on her elbow, looking despondent. "It makes no sense. Why would they raid a hospital?"

"Why would they raid the orphanage in Izieu?" asked Monsieur Lafleur. "Why would they slaughter those three hundred Italians in Rome? Because they can. That's why."

Vivienne rubbed her temples. "The officer suggested we try bribing the guards . . . but with what? We have no money."

"Ah!" said Madame Lafleur brightly. "With this, at least, we can help. We have some savings."

Vivienne looked startled. Then she burst into tears.

"Oh, Madame Lafleur! How can I ever repay you?" she asked.

Madame Lafleur waved her hand in the air as if wiping away the suspicions that had clouded the air between the two families for so long. "Quick, you must go now!" she urged. "These things cannot wait."

"I can drive," offered Monsieur Lafleur. "What's more, I know a shortcut. There's a military road through the mountains we can take."

"Please, can I come?" I begged. If Julien was in danger, I needed to go to him.

All three adults shook their heads. "Too risky, Sara," Vivienne told me. "You need to stay here, and stay out of view. I wouldn't even want you to return to the hayloft right now—it's too dangerous. Vincent's unit might come looking for him—his motorcycle is parked next to the barn, and for all we know, someone saw him go inside."

Frustrated, I returned to the window. I looked as far as I could, in the direction of the mountains, hoping in vain to catch a glimpse of my one true love.

As I looked out, something caught my eye. A small white bird, which bore a passing resemblance to—I reached into my pocket to confirm that it was still there and tightly closed my hand around it—the small carved bird Julien had made for me.

It felt like a sign. The good kind of sign: an omen, not a sign in a shop window telling me I was not welcome. This sign told me I was more than welcome. Follow me, the bird seemed to say, like birds in my dreams often would. So I closed my eyes and put all my wishes and prayers—indeed, my very soul— onto the wings of that small white bird.

Though the attic window remained as closed as my eyes, I felt myself taking flight. I soared over the mountains of the Mernuit. As I circled the area, I looked down below me.

I saw a winding road. And a truck. And soldiers beside it, standing guard at some sort of crossroads.

"Turn back," one of the guards told the truck's driver. "This road is closed."

"We're transporting prisoners to Aubervilliers," the driver replied.

The guard scoffed. "What idiot ordered that? There's no room for new prisoners! Who are they, anyway?"

"Sir, they're from the hospital in Dannevilliers. The facility needed to make room for wounded Germans."

The guard swore under his breath. Then he told the driver, "Get rid of them—quickly!"

"Okay, everybody out! Everybody out! Out! Hurry up!"

I circled lower. The truck was open at the back, and I could hear the prisoners talking among themselves.

"Wait, this isn't Aubervilliers," said one man, who remained seated. "Why are we getting out?"

"They told us we were being transferred to a better hospital," another man added.

"This road is blocked," the driver replied. "We have to take a long detour, and the commander wants you to take a bathroom break. Get out."

The prisoners looked at each other. Slowly, they began to climb off the back of the truck. One of the last ones off, I could see, was Julien. He was holding a crutch and being lowered down by two other prisoners. I felt a surge of joy and relief at the sight of his face, and I tried to keep him in view at all times. It was hard because of all the soldiers and their guns. I caught at least one looking like he wanted to take a shot at me.

"Follow me!" a guard ordered the prisoners. "Do not attempt to flee or you will be shot."

Julien and the two men who had helped him down exchanged worried glances.

"It's so obvious they're going to shoot us," whispered one of the men. "Might as well make a break for it."

The other man nodded in agreement. "If we all run at once, some of us might get away."

"You two! Stop whispering!" yelled a guard, pointing his rifle at them.

With armed guards at the front and back, the group was marched into the woods.

"Walk to the thicket up ahead," one of the guards at the back ordered. "You can do your business there."

"We're making a run for it," one of the men whispered to someone else in the group. "Pass it on."

"No talking!" screamed a guard at the front.

Two of the guards in the back exchanged disparaging looks. "Where'd they find these sorry misfits, anyway?" one asked the other.

"Most of them came from the loony bin" was the other guard's reply. He got a laugh in return.

"Good target practice, eh?" said the first guard, raising his rifle.

I didn't need to hear any more. At the risk of becoming a target myself, I lowered my head and swooped down. I hovered carefully, positioning myself just behind Julien's right ear.

Julien, can you hear me? I whispered.

I fluttered higher, surveying the situation. Could I do anything to distract the guards? Perhaps, but if they shot me, my efforts would have been in vain. I glanced around, hoping to see Monsieur Lafleur's car come into view. Certainly they were rushing to be here. Yet they were nowhere in sight.

But looking down, I saw that the prisoners were reaching an overgrown patch of bluebells, which gave me an idea. I dropped back down to Julien.

How high will you fly? I asked him.

No response. Perhaps he didn't even notice I was there. Frustrated, I darted in front of him.

"As high as the sky," I heard him say softly.

"Hurry up now!" yelled a guard, gesturing with his rifle. "To the thicket! To the thicket!"

The prisoners quickened their pace. But at the same time, a murmur of conversation went through them. I heard a man instruct the others, "When I say 'run,' run."

How fast will you go? I asked, hovering above Julien's head.

"As fast as a crow," he replied.

"A little farther . . . ," muttered the man organizing the escape. Julien did not appear to be listening to him. He was at the back of the pack, hobbling along with a single crutch.

Just then I heard the sound of a car approaching. Monsieur Lafleur! I circled back to try to tell them to hurry. I swooped down, hoping the sight of me would be enough. But I wasn't sure Vivienne and Monsieur Lafleur noticed me. They were in conversation with the guards and appeared to be at an impasse.

"The road is closed," they were told. "Turn around."

"But I have money for my son's release!" begged Vivienne from the passenger seat.

The guards exchanged a quick look. One winked and the other one held out his hand. "Give it here." When Vivienne passed him the money, the guard pocketed it and waved to the other soldiers. "Okay, let her through."

Vivienne and Monsieur Lafleur looked at each other. The

road was still blocked, so the guard's meaning was clearly that she should proceed on foot. Alone.

Vivienne got out of the car and began to walk around the military convoy truck. She looked unsure of where to go. A soldier called out to her.

"They took them into the woods," he said. "But you shouldn't—"

Something about his tone of voice made Vivienne turn and begin to run toward the forest. "Wait! Please!" she cried, even though she was nowhere near the group.

I knew it was up to me. I flew back to Julien.

Then close your eyes. . . .

Julien finished my thought: ". . . Time to rise."

I heard the sickening click of a guard's gun. It was now or never.

Everything began to happen at once.

I flapped my wings, beating them as hard as I possibly could to lift not only my small body but what felt like the weight of the world. A man yelled, "Run," and the prisoners began to scatter in all directions, trying to get away from their captors. There was shuffling and yelling and chaos. . . .

RA-TAT-TAT-TAT-TAT-TAT-TAT-TAT!

And gunshots. So many gunshots, echoing through the forest.

RA-TAT-TAT-TAT-TAT-TAT-TAT!

RA-TAT-TAT-TAT-TAT-TAT-TAT-TAT-TAT-TAT-TAT-TAT-TAT-TAT-TAT-TAT-TAT-TAT-TAT-TAT-TAT-TAT-TAT-TAT-TAT-TAT-TAT-TAT!

"Noooo!" cried Vivienne at the sound of the bullets flying.

"Julien!!" I screamed hysterically. Madame Lafleur wrapped her arms around me, trying to comfort me, but it was no use. I was trapped in that attic with feet of clay, unable to do a single thing to help my beloved Julien. I cried and cried in her arms, inconsolable.

Somehow, Madame Lafleur got me into a chair, and we sat there together for a long time. In my lap, I held the little carved bird Julien had made me, petting it gently as if I could bring it to life with my touch.

"Don't lose hope," said Madame Lafleur.

But I shook my head. Because I knew. Somehow, I just knew. We were connected that way, so it was as if I had been there. And it felt as if a part of me had died, too. I closed my eyes in sadness and frustration. As Madame Lafleur tried her best to reassure me, I felt increasingly numb. I let her words wash over me. And in my head, I tried to replace the awful images my brain was concocting with more peaceful ones. I pictured Julien walking, gaining speed, and dashing—almost floating—in the forest, through the magical field of bluebells. Then I saw golden rays of light raking through the trees. The light found him and wrapped him in its embrace. Julien kept leaning forward, reaching, and something inside him began to separate and change. He had no wings, and yet his feet left the ground. It was as if his soul rose up, free of his body and all his earthly limitations, and took flight.

Free as a bird.

*　*　*

"They never found Julien's body," Grandmère told Julian. "Whether that was because the Nazis covered up their dirty deed or the forest buried one of its own, we'll never know."

"Wasn't there a grave?" Julian asked. "When you took us to see your village, didn't we go to a cemetery?"

Grandmère nodded. "There is a grave marker at the spot where Julien's parents are buried. And their marker is for Julien, too, even though the Nazis never admitted what they did to him. And even though Vivienne bribed a guard, they stopped her before she got to the woods. They sent her home, but she kept asking questions and trying to get to the bottom of Julien's disappearance. She found out later that the reason the roads were being cleared that day was to make way for a German battalion heading north from Mende. The battalion was headed to Normandy, to keep the Allies from landing on D-Day.

"But the Maquis attacked them. So the Germans launched a massive counterattack. They bombed the woods and the villages around the woods. The maquisards were outnumbered ten to one. They fought bravely. But over two hundred of them died in the mountains. Many of their bodies, like Julien's, were never found. Vivienne also discovered that the other men on the truck with Julien had been taken from a mental hospital. They were memorialized with a plaque after the war. Julien's name was not put on the plaque, since it could not be proven he was there. But I knew, and so did Vivienne."

CHAPTER FIVE
Late Spring 1944–January 1946 . . . and Beyond

"Sara? Sara!" Vivienne called as she returned home from the market. I ran downstairs to greet her. Now that my hiding place had been shifted from the barn to the house, I could move about slightly more freely. I could even go into the Lafleurs' apartment. But mostly I stayed out of view, because one never knew when soldiers might arrive unannounced.

"I ran into an old friend," said Vivienne breathlessly, "and she told me her sister was there when the soldiers arrested Julien. She also said she's heard rumors that a lot of Jews are being hidden in the town of Le Chambon-sur-Lignon. So it occurred to me that perhaps, if Julien escaped . . ."

"But wouldn't he try to contact us?" I asked gently. While I believed in my heart that Julien was gone, I didn't want to rob Vivienne of her hope. It was all she and Jean-Paul had left.

"Perhaps," she allowed. "But if he was wounded, he might not be able to."

"I suppose that's true," I said.

She sat down wearily at the kitchen table. "I just wish they had let me go to him."

She said this often. It seemed like this was, for her, the hardest part about what had happened to Julien—that she was so close to him when the shooting broke out, and yet she was unable to save her child.

"If they had, neither of you might have survived," I pointed out, sitting down beside her.

Vivienne looked at me, her eyes filled with tears. "To hear them tell it, a shooting didn't even take place," she said bitterly. "What kind of monster denies a mother the chance to go to her child?" she asked.

I had no answer, so instead I reached for her hand. Her shoulders slumped and she leaned into me, letting me put an arm around her as she had done for me so many times.

"I begged them to let me go," she continued. "I told them he might be wounded, he might need me. They had the audacity to look me in the eye and claim that nothing had happened— even as the smoke was still in the air from their guns. 'Go home, madame,' they said. 'Drive away and don't come back.'"

"I'll make you some tea," I offered. Because that was all I could do on that day, and many of the days that followed. I would sit with her, listen to her wail in pain and frustration, and wait for Jean-Paul to come home from work. While he also held out hope for Julien's return, I could see in his eyes that he was more realistic. Like Vivienne, he refused to give up trying to find his son, but he seemed to do it out of a sense of duty rather than a belief that he would succeed.

*   *   *

"Sara, are you asleep?" asked Jean-Paul one evening, many months later.

"Not yet," I answered. It was a chilly night in November 1945, and the truth was that I had been having trouble sleeping. Not just that particular night, but for quite some time. Vivienne had brought extra blankets up to my attic room, but I couldn't bring myself to tell her that the problem wasn't the temperature. I was going through a prolonged rough patch, even though anyone looking at my situation would have thought things were greatly improved.

The war was over. It had gone on for so long, and it felt disorienting to see it end so quickly. First France was liberated in August 1944, which meant I could come out of hiding. But I still didn't go out. Months dragged on as I lived in a strange sort of fog. No longer a hidden girl, but still not ready to resume "regular" life—if I even knew what that was anymore. The Beaumiers and the Lafleurs were patient and kind, thankfully. They knew what I had been through and didn't rush me to move past my sadness and heartache. I'm not sure how I would have survived without them.

Then, in early May 1945, Radio London broadcast the official report that Germany had surrendered. I almost didn't believe it until I saw it in writing on the front page of the newspaper. Madame Lafleur said she was going to frame it—that's how happy she was. The end of the war meant I could return to school and be with Mariann and Sophie and the rest of my friends again. All of this should have made my fifteenth birthday, in late May 1945, a day for rejoicing.

But I didn't feel like celebrating, not on my birthday or for a long time afterward. Everything seemed different and wrong. All around me, and inside me, too. It was like I had a giant hole in my heart. And on cold evenings, like that night in November, I would lie awake and feel an unsettling breeze blowing clear through me, even under a pile of blankets. I didn't know how to bounce back or move forward or whatever I was supposed to be doing. I kept reminding myself that I should be grateful to be alive. Instead, I just felt sad and empty.

Jean-Paul came into my attic room, accompanied by Vivienne.

"We have some good news for you," Vivienne told me. She held out a folded piece of paper. It was yellow with red writing on it, and I instantly recognized it as a telegram. I knew that telegrams were expensive, so people only sent them with important news. But we already knew that the war had ended. And I could think of only one other reason for sending a telegram, so I looked at her, perplexed.

"I don't know anyone expecting a baby," I said.

"It's from your father," she replied, the corners of her mouth turning up.

Sara,

I have been searching for you. Nearly gave up hope. Many lists, many names! Day of roundup, Nazis came to my work, but I hid in forest. Snuck home. Waited a week for you and Maman, but not safe, so hid again. Maquis found me and smuggled me to Switzerland. Stayed for rest of war. Moved to Paris and now work at hospital. Spend all my time looking for you, my little bird. Today, learned of your whereabouts. Making arrangements now. Cannot wait to see you again.

Your loving Papa

"He's alive?" I marveled, reading the telegram again and again and hugging it to my chest even though I knew his hands had not touched it. Until that moment, it felt like the war had stolen and destroyed everyone I had ever loved. To have my father returned to me was the greatest gift imaginable.

I suddenly realized I was no longer shivering. It was as if that telegram had lit a spark inside me, giving me a purpose to live: so I could see my father again.

When he finally arrived on the Beaumiers' doorstep, it was like dry kindling reacting to that spark. It burst into flame. I cannot describe what it was like to be reunited with my father. Sometimes, there are no words.

He stayed with the Beaumiers for several days and spent time with the Lafleurs as well. There was so much to learn and catch up on, in our lives and in the world. Many of the horrors were truly unfathomable. We had known that the Nazis were heartless murderers, but it was not until the end of the war that we learned they had killed millions of people, including six million Jews.

"Among them my sister and her family," said Papa, shaking his head sadly.

"Yes. And my friends from the École Lafayette," I added.

And then we sat quietly and did not say the one that hurt most of all: my beautiful maman.

In January 1946, Papa packed his suitcase to return to Paris. And I got ready to go with him.

"Thank you again for all you have done for Sara," Papa told Jean-Paul and Vivienne. Papa and Jean-Paul shook hands formally.

"No need to thank us," replied Jean-Paul.

I stood there awkwardly, holding the suitcase the Beaumiers had given me and helped me pack. In theory I was ready to live with Papa. And yet I felt totally unprepared to say farewell to the Beaumiers. Jean-Paul had been so kind, and Vivienne had become like a second mother to me.

"I . . . I'm going to miss you so much," I said finally.

Vivienne leaned into a hug, closing her eyes and touching her forehead to mine. "You will always have a home here with us," she whispered. It was precisely what I needed to hear. Just as Julien would always live in my heart, a part of me would stay here with his parents, always.

And so, without a moment's thought, my hands went to the yellow scarf around my neck. The one I had always worn since Mademoiselle Petitjean had given it to me. Our foreheads were still touching, and in one smooth move I lifted the loop up over my head and put it around Vivienne's neck instead.

Vivienne brought her hand to the scarf. With tears in her eyes, she addressed me. "I will treasure it always."

Years later, the phone rang in the Beaumiers' house. I know because I was the one who placed the call.

"Allô?" said Vivienne sleepily.

"Sorry to call so early," I said. "I thought about sending a telegram, but . . ."

"Sara!" she replied excitedly. "Does that mean what I think it means?"

I laughed. "Yes. It's a boy."

"A boy!" exclaimed Vivienne. I heard her tell Jean-Paul, "It's Sara. She had the baby, and it's a boy!" Her voice had so much joy, you would think it was the birth of her own grandson. And in a way, it was. After all, I was like the daughter she never had. And after I left for Paris with Papa, I came back and visited them every summer—even when I was a grown woman.

"Do you remember what I told you at my wedding?" I asked her.

"Of course," said Vivienne. I knew she was remembering that happy day when she and Jean-Paul, along with Papa, had walked me down the aisle. "Is everything good? Are all of you doing okay?"

"We're wonderful," I told her, shifting the phone as my husband passed our sleeping infant back to me. "And we can't wait for you to meet . . . Julian."

"Oh!" Vivienne cried out, even though this was exactly what I had promised her I would do if I were ever blessed with a son.

As I hung up the phone, the baby stirred in his sleep. I lifted him onto my shoulder and walked with him to the rocking chair. I sat down and hummed softly to him while I looked out the window and watched the sun start to come up.

"Those are your other grandparents, Julian," I told him. "They were there for me when I needed them, and I will never forget their kindness." He nuzzled into my neck and I smiled. "You just got here," I told him, "but as you grow, you'll find that kindness, like love, stays with you forever."

I took a deep breath, smelling his sweet baby scent and feeling calm and safe in a way I had never thought I could feel again. "You see, Julian," I told him, "it always takes courage to be kind. But when you go through a time when kindness could cost you everything—your freedom, your life—kindness becomes a miracle. It is everything, kindness. It's a light in the darkness. It's the very essence of our humanity. It's hope."

"Are you teaching him poetry, Sara?" my husband asked, a bemused smile on his face.

I shook my head. "Just telling him how I feel."

He handed me a glass of water. "Look, there's that bird again," he said.

I took a sip, then turned and caught the tiniest glimpse of wings before the bird fluttered off. But as I gazed down at my sleeping child, I realized I didn't need to see it.

I already knew he was there with me. He always was.

EPILOGUE

What is done cannot be undone, but one
can prevent it from happening again.
—Anne Frank

PRESENT DAY

"And that, mon cher, is the end of my story."

For a moment there was silence on the other end of the phone.

Then Julian's voice came through, haltingly. "Oh, Grandmère, I don't know what to say. It's so horrible what happened to you . . . to Julien . . . to all those people."

"Yes," his grandmother said simply. She felt thoroughly drained. But also lighter, somehow.

Julian stared at her, still reeling from the impact of everything she had shared. "I don't understand," he said finally. "H-h-how could it have happened? How could six million Jews be killed in the Holocaust, and the world did nothing?"

"It's almost impossible to answer that question, Julian," replied Grandmère. "I think, in the end, it is like Vivienne told Pastor Luc. 'Evil will only be stopped when good people decide to put an end to it.' There must be the will. The struggle follows. Does that make sense?"

"I think so, Grandmère. In other words, people have to rise up."

"Exactly," she agreed. "Many brave souls—Jews and gentiles—

risked their lives to stand up against evil. But now, almost all of us who remember those days are gone. Vivienne and Jean-Paul died more than thirty years ago. That is why it is so important that your generation knows what happened to my generation, so that you will never let something like that happen again."

Julian nodded.

"You must promise me, mon cher. You will never let the world forget. If you see injustice, you will fight it. You will speak out. Promise me, Julian."

"I promise, Grandmère. I will never let them forget. I will shine my light . . . for you."

His grandmother sighed, grateful to see him so moved. Her friends often complained about how hard it was to get through to their grandchildren, how these young people were glued to their beloved screens. How ironic, Grandmère thought, that with her own grandson screens had not proved to be a barrier to connection and communication. Rather, in this case, screens were what facilitated it.

"Oh, mon cher," she told Julian, "you have no idea how happy you have made me."

"Grandmère? I love you. I'm so proud to be your grandson."

"Thank you, Julian," she told him. "I love you, too. More than words can say. Remember, you carry the name of the kindest person I have ever known. Good night, mon cher!"

"Good night, Grandmère. Sweet dreams!"

"You too, darling boy."

Grandmère hung up the phone. She felt pleased that she had done what she'd set out to do. Going back to those memories reminded her of how much loss and pain she had suffered, especially when she was so very young. But it also reminded her of all the beauty she was able to glimpse, even during the darkest of times.

She reached across her desk and groped around until her hand found a little wooden treasure chest. She had bought it when she was pregnant with her son, selecting it with a very specific purpose in mind. She pulled it closer and opened the lid, revealing several layers of light tissue paper. After reaching in and rustling the tissue paper aside, she withdrew the small treasure nestled within.

"Hello, my little bird," she said to the tiny wooden creature.

Though her hands had aged—alas, like the rest of me, she thought ruefully—that little carved bird still fit perfectly into the curve of her palm. Over the years, the wood had gotten smoother and shinier from the oils on her fingers. It remained her talisman, and she took it out and held it often. It never failed to bring her a sense of peace when she needed it the most.

About a month later, Grandmère was having her daily café et croissant (chocolate, of course) while reading the newspaper. She skimmed the style section and the arts section before turning to the international news. The image, and accompanying headline, made her stomach turn and her heart sink.

"No, no, no," she muttered to herself, as she found herself doing all too often. "It cannot be."

As she dug into the articles, her anger grew. Policies based on prejudice, indifference to the suffering of children, refugees in crisis, and a global rise in xenophobia and anti-Semitism.

"How can this be happening?" she wondered out loud. "Have we learned nothing?"

She took off her glasses and wiped her eyes in frustration. Increasingly, it was hard to even look at the news. She felt voiceless, powerless, frustrated, and afraid.

... tap tap ...

A light rapping noise at her kitchen window interrupted her thoughts. It came again.

... tap tap tap tap tap tap ...

"Hmm?"

Finally, she turned toward the sound.

Outside her window, in the middle of Paris, she saw a bird.

Not a pigeon, or a dove, or any of the birds one might expect to see outside the balcony of a Paris apartment. A little white bird.

A little white bird that looked her in the eye before quickly darting away.

But even in that briefest of moments, she knew what it was.

Or rather, who it was.

Grandmère smiled and closed her eyes. She felt the warmth of its wings beating in her heart.

She felt herself rise up with it and soar high above the city. She circled la Tour Eiffel, then let the air currents guide her out over the sea, dipping and gliding all the way until the Statue of Liberty came into view. From there, she turned north, her eyes fixed on a pulsing mass of people filling the streets. She swooped down and took in the grand spectacle of it. So many different people, all united in purpose, waving signs, singing, chanting, and marching together, their positive energy lifting her spirits and their energetic voices breathing hope into her lungs.

And one familiar young voice rising above them all.

*   *   *

"Grandmère, guess what! I went to a peace march today!" Julian announced excitedly when his grandmother answered the phone that evening. "It was amazing—there were so many people, all taking a stand against injustice. You would have loved it. You should have been there!"

"Tell me more, mon cher," she replied. "So I can feel like I was."

Grandmère picked up her little carved bird. She cradled it in the palm of her hand while her grandson told her all about the demonstration he had attended.

And as she listened, her heart took flight.

AFTERWORD

by Ruth Franklin

Most of *White Bird* takes place in France during World War II, but there's a scene early on that could happen in any school today. Sara, a budding artist who likes to doodle during class, has dropped her precious sketchbook. Her seatmate, who picks it up after class has let out, is a boy whose legs were twisted by polio; because of his sideways gait, their classmates call him by the cruel nickname Tourteau, or Crab. (His real name, as many readers will already know, is Julien.) Sara doesn't join in their teasing, but she also doesn't try to befriend him or speak up in his defense: she is a bystander. As he approaches her, balancing carefully on crutches, her friends start to whisper. "Eww. What does he want?" "I can smell him from here." (Julien's father is a sewer worker.) Sara thanks him for the sketchbook but doesn't object to her friends' cruelty.

Anyone who has read "The Julian Chapter" in *Auggie & Me,* in which R. J. Palacio fleshes out the backstories of some characters from her groundbreaking novel *Wonder,* will remember this boy and the role he comes to play in the life of not only Sara but also her grandson, Julian, his namesake. *White Bird* both continues and expands on that story, beginning—in a perfectly modern touch—with a FaceTime call in which the present-day Julian asks his grandmother to tell him more about her experience as a Jewish child in France during the war. Through her eyes, we see the Nazi menace as it gradually encroaches: the swastikas flying from the village buildings, the laws banning Jews from certain public places and requiring them to wear a yellow star, the first terrifying roundups and deportations. But for Sara, whose family lives in the Free Zone, life continues mostly as normal—until Nazis arrive at her school to round up all the Jewish children.

Like Lois Lowry's *Number the Stars, White Bird* is a fictional—though historically based—story of a child in hiding and the heroism of those who come to her aid. Notably, the book is not told from the point of view of the non-Jewish helpers, as is far more common in Holocaust literature for children and young adults, but from the perspective of the hidden child herself. *White Bird*'s message, too, is very much its own. "Evil will only be stopped when good people decide to put an end to it," says Vivienne, Julien's mother. For her part, Sara will come to understand—and deeply regret—her own moral crime in not standing up to her classmates as they bullied Julien.

When Sara apologizes to Julien, he consoles her: "The truth is, it doesn't matter how you used to be. It only matters how you are now." It's a message that everyone can relate to: Which of us has not, at some point, been a bystander to someone else's pain? The stakes in our own lives aren't usually as high as they are for Sara and Julien, but we never know when that might change. While we can't undo pain that we have caused, we *can* act differently in the future.

Holocaust survivor Elie Wiesel often quoted a line from Leviticus: "Do not stand idly by while your neighbor's blood is shed." Research has demonstrated that the Holocaust could not have taken place without the passive participation of millions of ordinary people who looked the other way as the Nazis exterminated their Jewish neighbors. But it's also true that the good deeds of those who saved the lives of their friends and fellow citizens—many of whom are honored by Yad Vashem, Israel's Holocaust memorial and research center, as "the Righteous Among the Nations"—are valuable beyond measure. Jewish tradition teaches that if someone saves a single life, it is as if they saved an entire world.

White Bird ends with a call to resist contemporary manifestations of prejudice and xenophobia. One needn't necessarily agree with the direct line the book draws from Nazi Germany to current events to be moved by its encouragement to stand up against tyranny and cruelty wherever we may find them, from the treatment of refugees to the tormenting of a disabled child in school. Sara's story has the power to transform her grandson from a bully into an ally. It might transform you, too.

Ruth Franklin is a book critic and the author of *A Thousand Darknesses: Lies and Truth in Holocaust Fiction* and *Shirley Jackson: A Rather Haunted Life*.

AUTHOR'S NOTE

Those who cannot remember the past are condemned to repeat it.

—George Santayana

The first time I heard this quote, which I use at the beginning of *White Bird,* was in my seventh-grade English class. We had just finished reading *The Diary of Anne Frank,* and my teacher, Ms. Waxelbaum, read the quote aloud as part of our discussion of the book. It has always stayed with me. So has the book. In fact, I would say that of all the books I've read in my life, *The Diary of Anne Frank* is the one that has had the greatest effect on me, not just as a writer, but as a person. *The Diary of Anne Frank* is one of the reasons I wrote this book.

Another reason—far more subtle—was a book I came across in a bookstore when I was nine years old. (It was actually the first "grown-up book" I ever purchased for myself.) It was called *The Best of LIFE,* and it was a large coffee-table book of photographs from the archives of *LIFE* magazine. *The Best of LIFE* was, in many ways, my introduction to the history of the world. It was from its pages of captioned photographs that I learned about the World Wars and the Vietnam War, the Cold War and the space race, Hiroshima and the atom bomb. I saw photographs of the civil rights movement, peaceful marches, hippies, famous people and ordinary citizens, visionary leaders and dictators. But the photographs I remember the most, too devastating to describe here, were of the concentration camps. Until then, I'd never heard of the Holocaust. Not at school. Not at home. All I knew about Nazis was from *The Sound of Music* and a TV show called *Hogan's Heroes*—which is to say I knew nothing.

That was not the case for my husband. He will tell you, as a Jewish man, that there was never a time in his life in which he did *not* know about the Holocaust. All of his mother's aunts, uncles, grandparents, and cousins had died in the Shoah (the Hebrew term for the Holocaust). It was an ever-present reality for her. It was an ever-present reality for almost every family in their predominantly Jewish neighborhood. It was taught in Hebrew school and Sunday school. It was discussed in temple. Just about everyone my husband grew up with had at least one relative—and sometimes an entire branch of the family—who had perished in the Holocaust.

In America today, there are children who may know a lot about the Holocaust, like my husband did, or very little, like I did. It's understandable that there would be a gap in what some kids know and some kids don't. The Holocaust, and the events leading up to the annihilation of six million Jewish people, is an extremely difficult subject to grapple with, whether you're an adult or a child. Most schools don't teach the subject until the seventh or eighth grade, if even then. This was explained to me by my husband's uncle Bernard, a New York City principal for many years, who was the first to suggest that the story of Grandmère, which I introduced in "The Julian Chapter," was the "perfect introduction"—his words—to the Holocaust. This is yet another reason why I wrote *White Bird*. (Thank you, Bernard!)

Although I did not know a lot about the Holocaust as a child, I've studied it a great deal as an adult, even before I wrote this book. It's a subject I think about often, which may seem odd to some people because, although I'm married to a Jewish man, I'm not Jewish myself. I know there may be some people who question whether I even have the right to tell this story, fictional as it is, because the Holocaust is not my story to tell. My feeling is that it should not fall solely on the victims of the Holocaust and their descendants to tell the story of the Holocaust. It should fall on everyone to remember, to teach, to mourn the loss. The millions of innocent people who died were the ultimate victims, but it was humanity itself—the very essence of who and what we are as human beings—that was attacked. It's not for Jewish people to stop anti-Semitism, after all—it's for the people who aren't Jewish to stop it in its tracks whenever they see it. That goes for any group that is discriminated against: the preservation of what is good and decent in our society falls on *all* of us.

That is what I believe, in any case, and why I made this book. To me, the heartbreak of a little girl, separated from her parents, forced to flee, living in fear of capture, is extraordinarily relevant at this moment in history. There are connections to be made between the past and the present. There are things we must always resist, wherever and however we can. I am a storyteller, so *White Bird* was my act of resistance for these times.

That the Holocaust took place, that people and nations let it happen, is something we should always struggle with, talk about, and learn from, so that we can make sure it never, ever happens again. Not on our watch.

A NOTE ABOUT THE DEDICATION

This book is dedicated to my mother-in-law, Mollie (Malka), whose parents, Max (Motel Chaim) and Rose (Rojza Ruchla), immigrated to America from Poland in 1921. Like hundreds of thousands of Jewish immigrants fleeing persecution and poverty in their homeland, Max and Rose settled on New York's Lower East Side, which is where Mollie grew up.

Mollie's high school graduation portrait.

The rest of Max's and Rose's families—their parents, grandparents, siblings, aunts, uncles, cousins— all stayed behind in Poland. Max's family was from Maków Mazowiecki. Rose's lived not far away, in Wyszków. In 1939, when the Germans invaded Poland, that entire region was annexed by the Third Reich. Of the 3,000 Jews who lived in Maków before the war and the 9,000 Jews in Wyszków, none survived. We know this from archives that are carefully kept by organizations dedicated to preserving the names of the Jews who perished in the Holocaust. What we cannot know is the impact this must have had on Mollie's mother and father. But we can imagine.

We are, all of us, a collection of those who have come before. In my children, I see my husband. In my husband, I see his parents. In his parents, I see an infinite past. This book is for Mollie, a beautiful, kind woman, who loved to laugh and sing; for her ancestors, who I'm sure also loved to laugh and sing; and for her descendants, including my sons, who carry in them a lineage that goes back to the dawn of time, and a light that will never fade.

GLOSSARY

This book is a work of fiction. It was not based on any one person's story, but was influenced by the many inspiring stories I've read over the years about children who went into hiding during the Holocaust and the ordinary citizens who helped them.

Some young readers, after reading *White Bird*, may decide they don't want to learn anything more about the Holocaust right now, which is totally okay. Some kids may wish to find out a little more. For these kids, I've provided a short glossary of some of the terms and events referred to in the book, as well as brief descriptions of the real-life inspiration for some of the characters and situations depicted in the book.

Anti-Semitism

Anti-Semitism is defined as the hatred of Jews as a group, be it religious or ethnic, which is often accompanied by hostile or passive discrimination against Jewish people. Anti-Semitism can be traced back to the Middle Ages in Europe, when Jewish communities were targeted for persecution. Examples of anti-Semitism: In Spain in 1492, Jews were expelled from all Spanish territories unless they converted to Christianity; in Russia, starting in the nineteenth century, pogroms were organized by local authorities to loot Jewish homes and businesses. The worst manifestation of anti-Semitism came in the twentieth century, when the Nazis committed genocide—the deliberate killing of six million Jewish people (see the Holocaust).

The Beast of Gévaudan

My inspiration for the wolf of Sara's nightmares came from the stories of the Beast of Gévaudan. This was a man-eating wolf that was purported to have roamed the forests of the Margeride mountains in the eighteenth

An eighteenth-century engraving of the Beast of Gévaudan.

century. Eyewitness accounts describe the beast as having enormous teeth and a gigantic tail. In a span of three years, from 1764 to 1767, it was said that the Beast of Gévaudan had attacked and killed over 100 people, including many children.

Although no one could prove that the victims had all been killed by the same wolf, or even by a pack of wolves, the legend became such a phenomenon throughout France that hunting parties were organized to find and kill the beast. This may have been the inspiration for numerous folktales and stories that have sprung up over the centuries involving a wolf-like beast living in the woods or the mountains, like "Beauty and the Beast," the legend of the werewolves—*voirloups* in French—and even "Little Red Riding Hood." Recent forensic studies have led scientists to speculate that the true Beast of Gévaudan was, in fact, not a wolf but a lioness, an animal that eyewitnesses might not have even known existed in that part of the world.

Concentration Camps

Concentration camps are detainment centers used to house large concentrations of people who have been imprisoned indefinitely, without legal cause or judicial oversight. During World War II, the Germans kept millions of captives inside concentration camps within both Germany and German-occupied territories. Some concentration camps were work camps, where captives were used as forced labor. Others were extermination camps, where large numbers of people were killed in gas chambers.

In *White Bird*, Mademoiselle Petitjean is last seen en route to the camp in Pithiviers after being turned away from the camp in Beaune-la-Rolande. These two were transit

A group of child survivors at Auschwitz on the day of the concentration camp's liberation, January 27, 1945.

camps inside France in which prisoners were held before being deported to concentration camps farther east.

Sara's mother, Rose, is taken to the Drancy camp, which was another transit camp in France. From there, Rose was transferred to Auschwitz, the largest and most notorious of the concentration camps. Located in Poland, Auschwitz was both a labor camp and an extermination camp in which, historians estimate, over one million Jews were killed until its liberation in January 1945.

Deportations/Roundups in France

In *White Bird*, Sara's family stops receiving letters from their relatives in Paris after the roundup of Vel' d'Hiv.

The Vel' d'Hiv roundup occurred in May 1942. Over 13,000 Jews—including more than 4,000 children—were arrested and detained inside the Vélodrome d'Hiver stadium, and held without adequate food, water, or sanitation. From there, most were transported to concentration camps.

Although other roundups of foreign-born Jews had taken place in the Occupied Zone as part of the Vichy government's ongoing collaboration with Germany, the Vel' d'Hiv roundup is considered the worst for several reasons: 1. the number of people arrested; 2. its location in the heart of Paris; 3. the arrests, for the first time, of women and children along with men. By this time, the Vichy government had published its "Statute of the Jews," outlining the restrictions placed on Jews living in the Occupied Zone.

In *White Bird*, Max refers to the roundup of Marseille, which occurred in January 1943. This was notable because it took

The yellow Star of David badge that Jews were required to wear. This one is from 1941.

place in the Free Zone. Two thousand mostly foreign-born Jews were immediately deported to concentration camps, and over 30,000 Jews were forced to leave when the Germans set fire to that sector of the city.

The roundup depicted in *White Bird*, which results in the arrest of Sara's mother, is based on these well-documented roundups, as well as other, smaller ones that occurred after the Germans occupied the Free Zone in November 1942. Although the Vichy government never sanctioned the deportation of French-born Jews, it did allow the denaturalization of some Jews not born in France. Sara's parents, both born outside of France, may have ended up on a deportation list because of this.

The Diary of Anne Frank

Anne Frank was just ten years old when the Nazis invaded the Netherlands, where she lived with her parents and her older sister, Margot. As they did in every country they occupied, the Nazis began systematically oppressing the Jewish population. Anne's father, Otto, decided his family would hide

behind his business to avoid the roundups he knew would come. With the help of his former employee Miep Gies, the Frank family, along with members of the Van Pels family, moved into the tiny quarters. The families had to stay very quiet during the day. They relied on Miep to bring them food. For the two years they were in hiding, Anne kept a diary, recording her thoughts and feelings and documenting the daily routines and drastic difficulties of being imprisoned inside a tiny room.

In August 1944, the police were tipped off and the secret annex was discovered. Everyone living in the secret annex was arrested and sent to concentration camps. Anne, her sister, and her mother were deported to the concentration camp Auschwitz, and then Bergen-Belsen. They did not survive. Neither did anyone else from the annex, except Anne's father.

After the war ended, Otto returned to Amsterdam, and Miep gave him Anne's diary, which she had kept hidden from the Nazis. *The Diary of Anne Frank* has been published in over seventy languages and has made a lasting impression on millions of people around the world.

Anne Frank writing in a journal in 1940.

The French Resistance

When Nazi forces invaded France in June 1940, the French government surrendered to Germany and signed an armistice, agreeing to split France in half. The Occupied Zone would be run by Germany. The Unoccupied Zone, or Free Zone, would be run by a German-approved French government located in a town called Vichy.

Shortly after, a French general named Charles de Gaulle gave a radio speech from London that called on French citizens to resist the occupation. By then, many small resistance groups, made up of men and women from all over the country and from all different social and economic backgrounds, including students, academics, artists, writers, doctors, housewives, and clergy from every denomination, had already formed secretly all over France, intent on fighting the Nazi occupation in whatever way they could. De Gaulle's speech became a clarion call for these resisters, whose actions—both great and small—were collectively known as the French Resistance. In the beginning, there was no central authority governing the French Resistance, but eventually it became a network of organized activity under the leadership of Jean Moulin, a civil servant, who parachuted into the heart of France to unite the various resistance factions under de Gaulle's Free French banner. Moulin was eventually captured and died in Nazi custody.

Different groups within the Resistance focused on different objectives. Some helped rescue, hide, or smuggle Jews and political prisoners to safety. Some sabotaged rail lines or blew up bridges to stop the advancement of the Nazi forces. Some established secret communications with the Allied forces outside France. Some were spies or double

Members of the Maquis, a group within the French Resistance, study the mechanism and maintenance of weapons dropped by parachute into the Haute-Loire region in 1940.

agents. Some published clandestine underground newspapers. Some, like the Maquis, were guerrilla soldiers (see the Maquis).

Gendarmes

Gendarmes were officers of the French Armed Forces who served as policemen, especially in small towns and rural areas where the French National Police did not have a strong presence. *Gendarmes* were often sent to round up—or assist in the roundup of—foreign-born Jews and refugees across the country.

Grandmère

The character of Grandmère in *White Bird* is (like so many of the characters in my stories) a mash-up of different people I've known in my life. In the case of Grandmère, I had three people in mind as I was writing and developing the character. One was my mother-in-law, Mollie, who liked to tell long, detailed stories. The second was my friend Lisa, who served as my illustration model for Grandmère. The third was an old woman I never actually met myself, but kept envisioning as I was writing Grandmère.

This woman was someone I used to see when I was a student at the American University of Paris. I would ride the 92 bus line to my school on the avenue Bosquet, and almost every day she would get on at the Maréchal Juin stop. She was impossible not to notice; she had such an elegant, imperious air about her. And she was always—*always*—dressed to the nines. Such a fashionable lady! While she never acknowledged my existence (she coldly appraised my army jacket and clogs one day, which rendered me incapable of ever starting a conversation with her in my broken French), I do remember eavesdropping on her often. She had a striking voice and piercing gray eyes. One time, she got into a long conversation with another older woman, and she said: *"Moi, j'étais une fille frivole, mais quand les Allemands sont arrivés, tout a changé."* Translated, that means: "Me, I was a frivolous girl once, but when the Germans arrived, all that changed." Who knows why that one phrase has stuck with me all these years. Maybe it had to do with the sense of tragedy I felt inside those words, the endless possibilities of a story that I would never hear from her but could imagine for myself. But that one line, more than thirty years later, is what launched Grandmère for me.

The Holocaust

The Holocaust (from a Greek word meaning "burned whole") was the mass murder of six million Jewish people by the Nazis during World War II.

The Nazis were a political organization in Germany that started shortly after World War I. Their ideology, which was built on the premise of German superiority and a belief that people of the "Aryan race" (i.e.,

Northern European whites) were superior to other races, was not taken seriously at first. However, as national bitterness about the terms of Germany's surrender grew and the Nazi Party leader, Adolf Hitler, rose in popularity, the Nazis acquired power. Hitler used the country's economic hardships to stoke deep-seated anti-Semitism in its citizenry, blaming Jewish people for all of Germany's problems.

When Hitler became Germany's chancellor in 1933, he launched a series of measures, including boycotting Jewish businesses, banning Jewish students from attending schools and universities, and expelling Jewish officers from the army. In September 1935, he unveiled the Nuremberg Laws, which stated that only people of pure "German or kindred blood" could be citizens. This stripped Jews who had been born in Germany of all their rights as German citizens, making it easier for them to be persecuted.

In late 1941, German Jews who had not already fled were forced to live in ghettos, which were walled districts that separated

Children in the Dachau concentration camp on the day it was liberated, April 29, 1945, by U.S. troops.

Jews from the non-Jewish population. Eventually, the ghettos were liquidated and the Jews were deported to concentration camps (see Concentration Camps).

As the Nazi forces swept through the rest of Europe, the Jewish citizens in those occupied countries were also arrested and deported to concentration camps. As a result, millions of Jews from all over Europe were sent to concentration camps. The Nazis also targeted other groups, including the Romani people, persons with disabilities, and homosexuals.

By the time the Allied forces won the war in June 1945, six million Jews had been killed, or two out of every three Jews who had been living in Europe before the war. Also killed were an estimated 220,000 Romani, 200,000 people with disabilities, and an unknown number of the 5,000 to 15,000 homosexuals who had been imprisoned in concentration camps.

After the war, when the full extent of the horrors of the Holocaust became known, many Nazis were put on trial for crimes against humanity.

As for the survivors of the Holocaust, some returned to their homes and tried to rebuild their lives, as Max and Sara did in *White Bird.* Some survivors immigrated to the United States. And others went to Palestine, where, in 1948, the State of Israel was founded.

In 2005, the United Nations instituted an International Day of Commemoration to honor the victims of the Holocaust. They stated, "The Holocaust, which resulted in the murder of one-third of the Jewish people, along with countless members of other minorities, will forever be a warning to all people of the dangers of hatred, bigotry, racism and prejudice."

Juliette Usach, a physician and the director of the La Guespy children's home, sits with five boys beneath a sign for Le Chambon-sur-Lignon in 1943.

The Jewish Resistance

In *White Bird,* Rabbi Bernstein and his wife are smuggled out of Dannevilliers by the Armée Juive. This organization, founded in 1942 in the South of France, was a resistance group that helped Jews escape from France.

There were many underground resistance groups that formed all over Europe to fight the Nazis—either through insurrection within camps and ghettos or by joining armed groups like the Bielski partisans in Poland or the Maquis in France (see the Maquis).

Le Chambon-sur-Lignon

In *White Bird,* Sara and Julien live in neighboring villages in the heart of the Haute-Loire region of France. Although Aubervilliers-aux-Bois and Dannevilliers are fictional, they are based on a village

The Maquis on a French mountain trail in 1944.

mounted a vicious counterattack, including bombardment by planes, tanks, and heavy artillery.

In the end, the few thousand *maquisards* gathered at Mont Mouchet were vastly outnumbered by the 22,000 German soldiers. About 300 *maquisards* were killed in the Battle of Mont Mouchet, although it's possible there were many more deaths unrecorded in the mountains.

in France called Le Chambon-sur-Lignon, where thousands of Jews were hidden from the Nazis during the war. Its citizens provided shelter in their homes, schools, and churches, and even in barns, like the one Sara hid in. For their humanitarian efforts, they were collectively declared Righteous Among the Nations by Yad Vashem, the Holocaust memorial center in Israel.

The Maquis

In *White Bird*, a *maquisard* risks his life to help the Jewish children in the École Lafayette escape into the woods. Although this event is fictional, in real life the Maquis were Resistance fighters who lived deep in the woods and mountains, where the Nazis could not find them. This is why they were called "Maquis," which means "thicket." An individual fighter was known as a *maquisard*.

Shortly before D-Day, word went out that the Maquis were gathering forces at Mont Mouchet, with the objective of delaying the Nazi troops en route to Normandy. It is estimated that 3,000 *maquisards* assembled in the Margeride mountains and began launching their guerrilla attacks against the German forces. The Germans, however,

The Milice

The Milice was a pro-Nazi militia group created by the Vichy government to help fight the French Resistance. They acted as a paramilitary police force and worked closely with the Nazis. After the war, many of them were executed in retaliation for their murderous efforts on behalf of the Germans.

Muriel Rukeyser

Muriel Rukeyser was a Jewish American poet (1913–1980) who wrote about the human struggle for love and equity in times of peace and war. An avowed pacifist, she wrote poetry as a form of protest, highlighting social injustice and inequity. The title *White Bird* is taken from Rukeyser's poem "Fourth Elegy: The Refugees," which I used as the epigraph of this book. It comes from her collection of poems *Out of Silence*, as do the quotes at the beginning of the three parts.

"Never Again" and #WeRemember

"'Never again' becomes more than a slogan: It's a prayer, a promise, a vow . . . never again the glorification of base, ugly, dark violence." —Elie Wiesel

The phrase "Never again," which Julian has on his sign at a protest march at the end of the graphic novel version of *White Bird,* has been used by many Jewish institutions and organizations over the years, including the U.S. Holocaust Memorial Museum, to remind the world about the genocide committed against the Jews during the Holocaust, and to guard against future genocides ever happening in the world.

#WeRemember is a hashtag that was developed as part of the #WeRemember campaign, the world's largest Holocaust remembrance event, which is pledged to fight racism and to end xenophobia (see Organizations and Resources).

Bobby, a child suffering from polio, uses a cane and a brace in August 1947.

Persecution of Persons with Disabilities

When Vincent accosts Julien in the barn, he says some things that reveal his knowledge of a Nazi-instigated euthanasia program called T4. This program's main imperative was to kill or sterilize people with disabilities, either physical or mental, who—in Nazi ideology— were deemed "inferior" or "unworthy of life." An estimated 200,000 people were killed in Germany as part of the T4 Program.

While there was no equivalent policy in France, an estimated 45,000 patients in several mental asylums and hospitals were known to have died of starvation and/or inadequate care during World War II. Whether this was part of a Vichy-sanctioned eugenics program or happened under the directive of highly unethical medical directors is still debated among historians and academics in France.

Polio

In *White Bird,* Julien walks with crutches because his legs were weakened by polio, which he contracted as a young child. Polio was a dreaded infectious disease that killed or paralyzed millions of people—mostly children— in the first half of the twentieth century. Families lived in fear of the disease, as children who caught polio were often quarantined, or separated from their families and sent to live in sanatoriums to recover. While some children made full recoveries, many were paralyzed.

In the 1950s, Dr. Jonas Salk invented a vaccine to prevent the transmission of polio. Although the disease could be eradicated from the earth, it is still spread in certain areas of the world where children have no access to vaccines.

Reverend André Trocmé, Daniel Trocmé, and the École Nouvelle Cévenole

Even before the German occupation of France, Reverend André Trocmé had been using his

Reverend André Trocmé with his wife, Magda (date unknown).

The identification card photo of Daniel Trocmé in 1938.

pulpit to preach against Nazism to the townspeople of Le Chambon-sur-Lignon (see Le Chambon-sur-Lignon). The school he started with his wife, Magda, and another pastor named Édouard Theis was called the École Nouvelle Cévenole. It was a coeducational school founded on the principles of tolerance and equality, and was the inspiration for the École Lafayette in *White Bird*.

As Jewish refugees began fleeing south from the Occupied Zone, Reverend Trocmé and Magda, along with Pastor Theis and a schoolmaster named Roger Darcissac, helped organize the town's citizenry to hide the refugees from the Nazis and/or smuggle them to safety outside of France. For these efforts, André, Édouard, and Roger were arrested and sent to an internment camp inside France, though they were eventually released.

Reverend Trocmé served as my inspiration for Pastor Luc.

The inspiration for Mademoiselle Petitjean was Reverend Trocmé's nephew, Daniel Trocmé, a schoolmaster at a nearby school called Maison des Roches. In June 1943, when his school was raided by the Nazis, Daniel Trocmé chose to accompany the eighteen Jewish students who had been arrested, although he himself had not been detained. This act of self-sacrifice ultimately landed him in the Majdanek concentration camp, where he died less than a year later.

For their heroism in saving at least 3,500 Jews, André, Magda, and Daniel Trocmé were recognized by Yad Vashem as Righteous Among the Nations.

Yad Vashem

Yad Vashem, the World Holocaust Remembrance Center, is an organization whose purpose is to document, commemorate, and research the Holocaust, as well as educate people around the world about the events of the Shoah. The Righteous Among the Nations is an honor bestowed by Yad Vashem upon non-Jews who saved Jews during the Holocaust.

SUGGESTED READING LIST

Dauvillier, Loïc, Marc Lizano, and Greg Salsedo. *Hidden: A Child's Story of the Holocaust.* New York: First Second Books, 2014.

DeSaix, Deborah Durland, and Karen Gray Ruelle. *Hidden on the Mountain: Stories of Children Sheltered from the Nazis in Le Chambon.* New York: Holiday House, 2006.

Feldman, Gisèle Naichouler. *Saved by the Spirit of Lafayette.* Northville, MI: Ferne Press, 2008.

Frank, Anne. *The Diary of a Young Girl.* New York: Bantam, 1993.

Gleitzman, Morris. *Then.* New York: Square Fish, 2008.

Gruenbaum, Michael. *Somewhere There Is Still a Sun: A Memoir of the Holocaust.* New York: Aladdin, 2015.

Kustanowitz, Esther. *The Hidden Children of the Holocaust: Teens Who Hid from the Nazis.* New York: Rosen Publishing Group, 1999.

Laskier, Rutka. *Rutka's Notebook: A Voice from the Holocaust.* New York: Yad Vashem and Time Inc., 2008.

Leyson, Leon. *The Boy on the Wooden Box.* New York: Atheneum Books for Young Readers, 2013.

LeZotte, Ann Clare. *T4: A Novel in Verse.* Boston: Houghton Mifflin Company, 2008.

Lowry, Lois. *Number the Stars.* New York: HMH Books for Young Readers, 2011.

Mazzeo, Tilar J. *Irena's Children: Young Readers Edition: A True Story of Courage.* Adapted by Mary Cronk Farrell. New York: Margaret K. McElderry Books, 2017.

Wieviorka, Annette. *Auschwitz Explained to My Child.* New York: Marlowe & Company, 2002.

Wiviott, Meg. *Paper Hearts.* New York: Margaret K. McElderry Books, 2016.

Zullo, Allan. *Survivors: True Stories of Children in the Holocaust.* New York: Scholastic Paperbacks, 2005.

ORGANIZATIONS AND RESOURCES

There are many wonderful organizations and institutions dedicated to Holocaust education and combating anti-Semitism and intolerance. These are just a few.

ANNE FRANK CENTER FOR MUTUAL RESPECT
annefrank.com

ANNE FRANK HOUSE MUSEUM
annefrank.org

THE ANTI-DEFAMATION LEAGUE
ADL.org

AUSCHWITZ MEMORIAL AND MUSEUM
auschwitz.org
Resources for teachers:
auschwitz.org/en/education

THE FOUNDATION FOR THE
MEMORY OF THE SHOAH
fondationshoah.org

HOLOCAUST MEMORIAL & TOLERANCE
CENTER OF NASSAU COUNTY
hmtcli.org

IWITNESS
Stronger Than Hate
iwitness.usc.edu

UCL CENTRE FOR HOLOCAUST EDUCATION
holocausteducation.org.uk

UNITED STATES HOLOCAUST
MEMORIAL MUSEUM
ushmm.org
Resources for educators:
ushmm.org/educators
Resources for students:
encyclopedia.ushmm.org

USC SHOAH FOUNDATION
The Institute for Visual History and Education
sfi.usc.edu

BIBLIOGRAPHY

GENERAL HISTORY OF FRANCE, JEWS IN FRANCE, WORLD WAR II, AND THE GERMAN OCCUPATION

Gildea, Robert. *Marianne in Chains: Daily Life in the Heart of France During the German Occupation.* New York: Picador, 2004.

Lanzmann, Claude. *Shoah: The Complete Text of the Acclaimed Holocaust Film.* New York: Da Capo Press, 1995.

Marrus, Michael R., and Robert O. Paxton. *Vichy France and the Jews.* New York: Basic Books, 1981.

Rajsfus, Maurice. *The Vél d'Hiv Raid: The French Police at the Service of the Gestapo.* Translated by Levi Laub. Los Angeles: DoppelHouse Press, 2017.

Rosbottom, Ronald C. *When Paris Went Dark: The City of Light Under German Occupation, 1940–1944.* New York: Little, Brown and Company, 2014.

Vinen, Richard. *The Unfree French: Life Under the Occupation.* New Haven, CT: Yale University Press, 2006.

THE HOLOCAUST AND ANTI-SEMITISM

Gilbert, Martin. *The Holocaust: A History of the Jews of Europe During the Second World War.* New York: Henry Holt and Company, 1985.

Lazare, Lucien. *Rescue as Resistance: How Jewish Organizations Fought the Holocaust in France.* Translated by Jeffrey M. Green. New York: Columbia University Press, 1996.

BBC News. "Tel Aviv unveils first memorial to gay Holocaust victims." January 10, 2014. bbc.com/news/world-europe-25687190

Encyclopædia Britannica
britannica.com/event/Holocaust

Holocaust Encyclopedia
encyclopedia.ushmm.org/content/en/article/nazi-camps
encyclopedia.ushmm.org/content/en/article/introduction-to-the-holocaust
encyclopedia.ushmm.org/content/en/article/glossary

Montreal Holocaust Museum
museeholocauste.ca/en/history-holocaust

United States Holocaust Memorial Museum
ushmm.org

JEWS IN POLAND AND PERSONAL FAMILY HISTORY

Ancestry.com

JewishGen Inc. (affiliate of the Museum of Jewish Heritage, New York City) jewishgen.org

Virtual Shtetl (POLIN Museum of the History of Polish Jews) sztetl.org.pl/en

THE FRENCH RESISTANCE, THE MAQUIS, AND THE BATTLE OF MONT MOUCHET

Evans, Martin. "A History of the French Resistance: From de Gaulle's Call to Arms Against Vichy France to Liberation Four Years Later." *History Today* 68, no. 8 (August 2018). historytoday.com/reviews/history-french-resistance

Gildea, Robert. *Fighters in the Shadows: A New History of the French Resistance.* Cambridge, MA: Belknap Press, 2015.

Gueslin, André, ed. *De Vichy au Mont-Mouchet: L'Auvergne en guerre, 1939–1945.* Clermont-Ferrand, France: Institut d'Études du Massif Central, Université Blaise-Pascal, 1991.

Kedward, H. R. *In Search of the Maquis: Rural Resistance in Southern France, 1942–1944.* New York: Clarendon Press, 1993.

Sanitas, Jean. *Les tribulations d'un résistant auvergnat ordinaire: La 7e compagnie dans la bataille du Mont-Mouchet.* Paris: Éditions L'Harmattan, 1997.

Chemins de Mémoire: The Maquis du Mont Mouchet cheminsdememoire.gouv.fr/en/maquis-du-mont-mouchet

Chemins de Mémoire: The Resistance and the Networks cheminsdememoire.gouv.fr/en/resistance-and-networks

THE RIGHTEOUS AMONG THE NATIONS AND THE HIDING OF CHILDREN IN FRANCE

Bailly, Danielle, ed. *The Hidden Children of France, 1940–1945: Stories of Survival.* Albany, NY: State University of New York Press, 2010.

Flitterman-Lewis, Sandy. *Hidden Voices: Childhood, the Family, and Anti-Semitism in Occupation France.* Abondance, France: Éditions Ibex, 2004.

Gilbert, Martin. *The Righteous: The Unsung Heroes of the Holocaust.* New York: Henry Holt and Company, 2003.

Grose, Peter. *A Good Place to Hide: How One French Community Saved Thousands of Lives During World War II.* New York: Pegasus Books, 2015.

Jeruchim, Simon. *Hidden in France: A Boy's Journey Under the Nazi Occupation.* McKinleyville, CA: Fithian Press, 2001.

Klarsfeld, Serge. *The Children of Izieu: A Human Tragedy.* New York: Abrams, 1984.

Scheps Weinstein, Frida. *A Hidden Childhood: A Jewish Girl's Sanctuary in a French Convent, 1942–1945.* New York: Pegasus Books, 2015.

YAD VASHEM

Yad Vashem—The World Holocaust Remembrance Center yadvashem.org/righteous/resources/righteous-among-the-nations-in-france.html yadvashem.org/righteous/stories/trocme.html

swarthmore.edu/library/peace/DG100-150/dg107Trocme.htm

MURIEL RUKEYSER

Rukeyser, Muriel. *Out of Silence: Selected Poems.* Evanston, IL: Northwestern University Press, 1992.

THE BEAST OF GÉVAUDAN

Sánchez Romero, Gustavo, and S. R. Schwalb. *Beast: Werewolves, Serial Killers, and Man-Eaters: The Mystery of the Monsters of the Gévaudan.* New York: Skyhorse Publishing, 2016.

Smith, Jay M. *Monsters of the Gévaudan: The Making of a Beast.* Cambridge, MA: Harvard University Press, 2011.

Taake, Karl-Hans. "Solving the Mystery of the 18th-Century Killer 'Beast of Gévaudan.'" *National Geographic.* September 27, 2016. blog.nationalgeographic.org/2016/09/27/solving-the-mystery-of-the-18th-century-killer-beast-of-gevaudan

FRENCH PSYCHIATRIC HOSPITALS IN WORLD WAR II

Lafont, Max. *L'Extermination douce.* Lormont, France: La Bord de l'Eau, 2000.

von Bueltzingsloewen, Isabelle. "The Mentally Ill Who Died of Starvation in French Psychiatric Hospitals During the German Occupation in World War II." *Vingtième Siècle:* Revue d'histoire 2002/4, no. 76.

cairn.info/article.php?ID_ARTICLE=VING_076_0099

GLOSSARY IMAGE CREDITS

WHITE BIRD DISCUSSION GUIDE

1. *White Bird* begins with a conversation between Grandmère (Sara) and her grandson, Julian. At first, Grandmère is reluctant to share the story of what happened to her as a girl in Vichy France but eventually decides to open up. Why do you think it is important to share our personal stories?

2. Grandmère starts her story with the words "Once upon a time . . . ," a traditional beginning for fairy tales. How was her early life like a fairy tale?

3. Part One of *White Bird* opens with the following quote: "The birds know mountains that we have not dreamed." What does this statement mean to you? What role do birds play throughout the book?

4. After Sara asks why people hate them for being Jewish, her father reminds her that not all people hate them. She asks if the people who do are bad. He tells her that rather than seeing people as good or bad, he believes that people have a light inside them, but some have lost that light. "They have darkness inside them, so that is all they see in others: darkness." He continues, "Why do they hate us? Because they cannot see our light. Nor can they extinguish it. As long as we shine our light, we win." Think about his explanation. Do you agree? Do you believe that people who live in darkness can once again find their light? How? Can you help? Would you help if you could, knowing that it might put you at risk?

5. Take a moment to think about Sara's life in the barn. What are the biggest challenges of living in this space? Consider the actions of Julien, a boy who

has been cruelly called Tourteau ("crab") by his classmates. Why do you think he and his family risk their lives to hide Sara? Why is this decision a perfect example of the power of kindness to change hearts and save lives?

6. In describing her relationship with Julien, Sara states, "The best friendships are the ones in which words are not needed." Do you agree with this sentiment? How do you and your closest friends find ways to support each other without having to talk?

7. Drawing and creating art are instrumental in helping Sara make sense of the world. Examine how her drawings are used in the story. To what degree does Sara's art connect her to those she loves and to the world at large?

8. After her son is attacked by the school bully, Julien's mother, Vivienne, tells Pastor Luc, the school's principal, "Evil will only be stopped when good people decide to put an end to it. It is our fight, not God's." Do you agree with this statement? If so, how do you take action to stand up to injustice?

9. Despite Sara's harrowing circumstances, she manages to remain hopeful. Why do you think that is? What helps you to remain hopeful in difficult circumstances?

10. One of the most important takeaways from *White Bird* is captured in the following statement: "In these dark times, it's those small acts of kindness that keep us alive, after all. They remind us of our humanity." Why is actively choosing kindness so essential? Can you connect this message to events happening today?

11. Given the state of world affairs, why is remembering the Holocaust and examining current parallels more important than ever?

ACKNOWLEDGMENTS

It takes a village to make a book. This is always true with any type of book that gets published, but it was especially true of the original graphic novel of *White Bird,* which was published three years ago—and especially, ESPECIALLY true of this novel, written by the incomparable and amazing Erica S. Perl, which was based on that original.

It was my wonderful editor, Erin Clarke, who first suggested I write a novelization of my graphic novel. Despite the rising popularity of the graphic novel genre, "not everyone reads them, and the story of *White Bird* is worth getting out to as many people as possible," were Erin's words (more or less). I agreed, but I knew that I myself couldn't do it. The writer in me had already expended my creative energy on the graphic novel, and I didn't think that I could add more to it. In order to become something new, something great—which it would have to be if we were going to do this—it would need a new spark of creativity and a burst of new energy. And yes, a new approach.

Enter Erica S. Perl. I had met Erica at a writers' conference a few years before. I loved her sense of humor, and we immediately fell into that familiar speech of old friends, even though we'd only just met. Erin had edited Erica's previous books, so when she suggested we ask Erica to adapt the graphic novel to this format, it felt like destiny calling. I could not have asked for a more beautifully written adaptation of my story. Thank you, Erica S. Perl, for embarking on this labor of love. I know it was deeply emotional and personal for you and your family, and I feel blessed that you lent your enormous talent to this project. And thank you, Erin, for connecting us.

While Erica was writing this novel, the team at Lionsgate was very busy getting the film adaptation of *White Bird* under way. I, along with David Hoberman and Todd Lieberman, produced the movie, and Marc Forster, one of the most talented, in-demand directors of our day, agreed to helm the film, which was based on a screenplay by Mark Bomback. Marc, with the incomparable Renée Wolfe by his side, put together an incredible team to film in Prague, in the dead of winter, in the midst of lockdown, and they created what I personally think is one of the greatest movies about the Holocaust since *Schindler's List.* The cinematography, the lighting, the costumes, the production design, the set design—not to mention the acting—are at a level beyond anything I could have hoped for as the author of the work being adapted. The young leads, Ariella Glaser and Orlando Schwerdt, are mesmerizing. Bryce Gheisar reprises his role as Julian, which is an important loop to be closed for fans of the original *Wonder.* And, of course, Helen Mirren and Gillian Anderson, as Grandmère and Vivienne, respectively, are living legends for a reason. Thank you to all the abovementioned, and the entire cast and crew, for bringing your talents and energies to this movie, which is, sadly, so relevant and so needed at this moment in history.

Thank you to the colossal team at Random House, including Barbara Marcus, Felicia Frazier, Artie Bennett, April Ward, and all the researchers and fact-checkers who helped make this book. Thank you to Sarah Neilson for your careful review of the graphic novel, both art and text; and Dr. Elizabeth B. White and Edna Friedberg, PhD, from the United States Holocaust Memorial Museum, for your thorough examination of the historical events depicted.

Thank you to Alyssa Eisner Henkin.

Thank you to my husband, Russell, who is my partner in all things, and whose family I am so proud to be a part of. I know Mollie is looking down on you and smiling, Russell. And thank you to Caleb and Joseph, for reminding me every day that this world is worth fighting for.

A NOTE FROM ERICA S. PERL

I first picked up *White Bird* in the graphic novel section of my local independent bookstore. I began to flip through it . . . then found myself sitting on the floor, having been completely transported while reading it cover to cover. I was pleased when it won the Sydney Taylor Book Award, excited to learn it was being made into a film, and extremely honored to be asked to create a novel based on the graphic novel. I said yes immediately, not only because I loved the story but also because I felt such a strong connection to the material.

In 1937, Hans and Elizabeth Strauss fled Nazi Germany with their young son and five-month-old daughter. That baby girl grew up to be Maryann Strauss Sewell, an accomplished soprano and voice teacher, as well as the mother of my husband, Michael (Mike), and the grandmother of our girls, Francesca (Franny) and Beatrice (Bougie). While I am beyond grateful that Maryann and her immediate family were able to get out when they did, I know that many others were not so fortunate. There are entire branches of my own Jewish family tree that we will never know.

I dearly hope this book does justice to all Holocaust survivors and victims, as well as courageous friends and allies. I also hope that readers will come away with a renewed resolve to stop anti-Semitism and all forms of discrimination—work that is ongoing for all of us.

I am deeply thankful to R. J. Palacio for entrusting her incredible graphic novel to me and for being so generous with her thoughts, insights, and encouragement, as well as her research materials. Thank you also to Erin Clarke and the entire team at Random House and Knopf Books for Young Readers. Thank you to Carrie Hannigan and the whole HG Literary team. I also wish to thank Dr. Rebecca Erbelding of the United States Holocaust Memorial Museum. And I am grateful to the D.C. Commission on the Arts and Humanities, the Jewish Book Council, the Association of Jewish Libraries, and PJ Library for supporting my work. Many thanks to Tammar Stein, Katherine Marsh, and Caroline Hickey—wonderful critique partners as well as true friends—and also Kenna Kay, Sczerina Perot, Gary DiBianco, Elizabeth Lyster, Jenifer Marshall, Phineas Baxandall, Sarah Hill, Elizabeth Shreve, Alan Silberberg, and Erik D'Amato.

And last, but certainly not least, thank you to Mike, Franny, and Bougie.